P9-AGH-840

REFUGIO, THEY NAMED YOU WRONG

REFUGIO, THEY NAMED YOU WRONG

A NOVEL

BY
SUSAN CLARK SCHOFIELD

ALGONQUIN BOOKS OF CHAPEL HILL
1991

Published by
Algonquin Books of Chapel Hill
Post Office Box 2225
Chapel Hill, North Carolina 27515-2225

a division of
Workman Publishing Company, Inc.
708 Broadway
New York, New York 10003

Printed in the United States of America.

Library of Congress Cataloging-in-Publication Data
Schofield, Susan Clark, 1958–
Refugio, they named you wrong : a novel / by Susan Clark Schofield.
p. cm.
ISBN 0-945575-60-2
I. Title.
PS3569.C5253R44 1991
813′.54—dc20 90-21972
CIP

For Ande, Carol, Kim, and Lisa,
and for Jeff,
with love

I do not believe that any kind of riding will pump virtue into a man like that in pursuit of wild, strong, mighty-horned cattle plunging for liberty or just walking like phalanxes of destiny towards the tail end of the world.

—from *The Longhorns*
by J. Frank Dobie

Every man must kill his own snakes.

—Old Brush Country Saying

REFUGIO, THEY NAMED YOU WRONG

PART ONE

ONE

I look through the eyes of a rattler, tail up and rattles going like hail on a roof but Pa goes right on, never heeding my warning.

"Peter Jack! Peter Jack!" Guttural, calling me over and over: "Peter Jack! Peter Jack!"

Hail on a tin roof, hard hitting.

Hail like fists, like fists. Pa hitting Mick. Mick, guttural and anguished: "Peter Jack! Peter Jack!"

Looking out through rattler's eyes, round and black as bullets, looking out and Pa hits him again, hail as big as fists, Pa's fists, bunched up like Pa's face, screwed up face all red and eyes blue flames, brows together and screwed up, hair orange flames in the wind, blows jerk both bodies.

Mick calls, guttural and weaker: "Peter Jack. Peter Jack."

Coil tight inside my skin, dry skin looks wet, looks like speed itself. Coil tighter, tighter. Rattle held higher, hail on a tin roof, tat-tat-tat-tat all beating together, millions of hailstones fall like fists, like stars out of the sky, beat on the drum that is my brother's body. My brother Mick: "Peter Jack . . ."

On his knees, straw hair over his eyes, wet cheeks, wet over splotched red from hailing fists. Hands and knees, and I coil tighter. Fangs lie back in my mouth, back along the roof, start to drop; feel them against my tongue. Tongue snakes in and out, in and out, quivers on each out. Black bullet eyes never blink. Skin tighter and tighter, coil tighter.

Pa's right arm up, fist clenched, falls, crashes on my brother's back.

"Peter . . ."

Striking, snaking, full length, a bullet down the barrel of a gun, bursting, uncoiling, end of the barrel, jaws spring wide so wide, come apart, fangs drop, ready, drip with death. Straight for his neck, neck red and corded and so close now with rough scaly skin so close. Sink deep snap shut, plunge in and in. Meet inside his neck, snap against each other, blood spurts onto my face, no more dry snake: red and wet and slippery now. Pump that venom, pump it pump it pump it he's dead. Mick's dead Pa's dead he's dead they're dead.

My eyes fly open like the jaws of that snake and I lie on my back on the floor of the room at the back of the cantina, and Mercedes kneels, looking at me with her black eyes narrow and smug and damn if she don't know I had that dream again.

So she smiles a little, and her full lips curve up in her dark Mexican face, but she don't show her teeth because she has two bad ones near the front. She has curly black hair that looks red in the sun and falls clear past her waist, and it's back behind her shoulders now so her melon-round breasts show big above her fleshy belly, and she has her hands on her knees so her arms push her breasts together and the brown nipples point straight forward and her breasts look bigger than ever, shining with sweat.

But I don't look there, just know what I'd see if I did. I don't look anywhere, except maybe straight up at the mesquite poles that hold the thatched roof, and the brushy thatching sticking through the poles.

That snake dream crawls off into the Refugio County brush, all shot to hell, and I lie on my back on a piece of rawhide on a hard-packed dirt floor in San Fernando, Mexico, and it's fall of 1884 though you'd never know it was fall or morning from this God damn heat. Sweat prickles my face, feels like oil on my skin, trickles over my ribs and down my side, mats the hair on my chest, mats the hair on my head between me and the rawhide. Damn if it ain't too hot for this time of year.

"You will leave soon, Costello," says Mercedes, so I look at her.

"Not today." Don't come out right: choked. "Not today."

"*Yo sé. Pero mañana.*"

Tomorrow, right. Always tomorrow. And she always knows. Three years I've come here and she still knows ahead of me. Sold the cattle a month ago in the Dakotas, came right back and been here ever since with nary a thought of leaving, and now she up and knows just like I do: winter's on the way, even here, even with the hot sun coming across Refugio County on the Texas coast, across Live Oak County south of San Antone, across the Brasada where thorns weave crowns over Godforsaken ground and press in on prairies of mesquite grass and bushes and horse manadas with chasing, biting stallions; across Carrizo Springs and the Buckley outfit's herds of wet stock, across the Rio Grande and Don Vicente Renova's hacienda on the Mexican side and into San Fernando, here, with the monastery mirthless on its hill, watching us like the sun, which rolls in the open back door and over my naked body and makes me sweat.

I got no more love for San Fernando than any other place in Mexico or Texas or on Earth.

"How do you know when I will leave?" I ask in Spanish.

"In your eyes, in the tone of your voice: it is there. And in the way you make love to me. Always, I can tell."

Always, we speak Spanish. It keeps us apart.

"Getting on toward winter, that is how you know. Only from the season."

She smiles that smile again, without showing her teeth, with the corners of the lips tugging up and that smug sureness in her black eyes, and the eyelids half-closed, and you'd think she hated me but I know a whole lot better because it's the same from me to her: we're friends if you can get past the Spanish and the smugness and the way I come near hating her as much as San Fernando just before I leave. We're friends or she'd call me Jackson instead of Costello, my real name: Peter Jack Costello, not Pete Jackson. Peter Jack Costello, born Refugio County, 1858, 5′10″, 165 lbs., light hair, blue eyes, mustache, sometimes bearded, bullet scar right shoulder, wanted dead or alive for murder of Jack Costello, father, and Michael Costello, brother, $3,000 reward offered by mother: read it on the fucking wanted poster and you have it all.

Except it was my father killed my brother, not me.

Mercedes' room is small and clean except for the ticks that sometimes fall from the thatching after it's patched. She keeps the floor swept and the 'dobe walls whitewashed; there are a scrubwood washstand and chair and on the washstand a blue and white porcelain pitcher sits full of spring water in a matching basin, looking fragile and out of place and waiting for us to get as clean as the room. Might as well wait for the end of the world.

The washstand and chair are across from the door to out back. Last night Mercedes folded my buckskin shirt, deep-pocket vest, corduroy breeches, leather leggins, and longjohns and put them on the chair; my black flat-crowned Stetson and gunbelt with the Colt are hung over the back, my work spurs and fresh-blacked boots are on the floor by the leg, and I got no desire to put on any of it because of the heat.

I wish a breeze, even a hot breeze, would come in that door and dry this sweat, but that's a wish on the moon and a fly buzzes in instead. The fly lights on the rim of a tiny bowl of holy water tacked on the wall below a crucifix. Mercedes wraps herself in a cotton dress and throws a rebozo across her shoulders. Her hair sticks to her face and arms. She shoves it out of the way and waves the fly from the holy water.

I roll over and stare at the whitewashed wall that has sandy pink of adobe working through the white. Boring wall, but I'd rather stare at it than get dressed. Mostly I'd rather be somewhere else. Anywhere.

"You will act like this all day," says Mercedes. "All today and all tomorrow, until you leave. You should leave now and spare me this mood."

"Go to hell," I mutter.

She laughs tersely. She wants me to stay, that's how I see it.

"Joshua wants to go," I say.

She laughs again: "Ha!" Like that, never more. "Do not blame Chiso. He always wants to leave. He would never come here if not for you."

"And my Mexican whore."

"You are a complete bastard, Costello."

I roll onto my back. Rawhide has cooled where the air took up the sweat. Mercedes faces out the door, leans on one elbow, faces east to Don Vicente's and Texas and blocks the sun. She can stand there all day and make shade for me but she'd block the breeze too, if any decided to blow.

"Why do you call Joshua 'Chiso' but never me 'Jackson'?" I ask. As if I care: I want her to move.

"That is easy. Chiso is named for his mountains, for his *querencia.* You have no *querencia,* only this false name. A man should have the name of that which he loves, not one to hide behind. Chiso has his Chisos, you have only an alias."

Of course she hasn't moved.

"I have Texas."

Her body jerks but there's no laugh. "Texas. You do not love Texas and Texas will never love you. You have no *querencia* and that is that. Texas. Costello Texas. I might as well call you San Fernando, or Renova. Get up Costello, you need to leave."

But she wants me to stay, I know, because she pressed her body against mine when I stirred early this morning. She pressed all of her body against all of mine, not just the parts for sex; not a sexual touch but a clinging touch, and her skin against mine felt sticky and made me itch, so I moved away and went back to sleep. And had that dream.

Mercedes rustles behind me in the cantina, fixing coffee. I sit looking out the door to where horses' hooves and point-toed boots have loosed chunks of gravelly earth. Ain't nothing out there now but 'dobe huts, chickens, dogs, maybe a goat or two down the road, nothing but sun and San Fernando, smelling like dust and cookfire smoke and brush, faint enough that you can't smell it unless you stand right outside and take a deep snort, and then it only makes you sneeze. Sun's still behind the cantina, baking that back room, so the building makes a big gray shadow on the road, ends in a line sharper than a longhorn cow's hoof, so the sudden light beyond it makes you squint.

Mercedes pours a cafecito and sets it in front of me on a table that could give you splinters.

"*Quieres pulque?*" She holds up an olla full of the bitter milky white drink.

"Got any rum?"

"You and the vaqueros drank all of it last night. You and they and the floor."

"They did. Not me."

"*Sí.* Your bad humor kept you sober. Must be very bad, then, worse than ever."

I wave my hand toward her and she puts the pulque away. Hell with her. Coffee steams, bitter, burns my mouth like it should. Off somewhere a goat bleats, then a dog yaps, then I listen beyond them, beyond San Fernando, to what my ears don't hear but what I know is there, and Mercedes puts her hand on my shoulder from behind and I put my hand over hers and squeeze.

"Chiso," I say, when we can hear the hoofbeats for real. They pound louder and louder, come into town from the hacienda, draw the dogs to prance and yap at the horse's heels, drown the yapping or so it sounds, the triple beat of a canter, like a man drums his fingers on the table, like I drum mine, in time. Then a trot, one-two-one-two, and a walk, so now you can hear the creak of saddle leather and the dogs scuffle on the rocky road and the hooves barely move, finally don't move at all. Horse blows through his nostrils, tosses his head, shakes the tack in a slapping sound.

Joshua walks into the cantina. Half-French-Canadian from a trapper, half-Apache from a squaw, he's tall and lean with black hair that falls straight to his shoulders from under his hat with the snake-skin band. His skin is hard-polished red-brown; his eyes are secret and dark as the entrance to a blackrock cave, and he has a glossy corded scar that starts beside his left eye and hooks under his narrow slash of a mouth.

"Hell, why not sleep all day," I say to him.

"It's only an hour past dawn." He has a voice to match his eyes, voice like a blackrock cave.

We've rode together near four years, mostly around the border and some over to the Brasada, then splitting up every summer so I can trail a herd north for Don Vicente. We hooked up in a canyon in the Chisos Mountains where the Rio Grande takes its big turn; Joshua and an old Negro compadre from his outlawing days have a cabin and a bunch of honest-bought beef and horse stock there. Joshua's done about every kind of outlawing, but all I know comes from the Negro, Andy, because Joshua don't let on much. I never rode with their gang, never wanted that kind of life but also never had the chance, since they split up before I come back from up north. Truth is I never robbed no one in my life, just drove cows, mostly.

So Joshua takes a seat and Mercedes greets him kind of solemn-like, as she will when a man ain't one to talk. She brings him a cafecito while he rolls a shuck, and soon he holds the coffee cup in one hand close to his face so the steam catches up under his hat. Looks kind of eerie. He takes off the hat and draws on the shuck, and the scent from the cornhusk wrapper mixes with the scent of tobacco and coffee, then frijoles and tortillas coming from the stove, and finally the day's got started proper.

"How're the vaqueros this morning?" I ask.

"Not saying much."

I layer some beans on the tortilla and roll it. Beans drip from the other end onto the tin plate. Mercedes makes the hottest beans around, set a gringo to honking and snorting like an old locomotive. We ain't gringos, not exactly. I finish off four or five tortillas, start on a third cafecito: bottom of the pot, you could stand your leggins in it.

"Good coffee, Mercedes."

Joshua nods.

"*Gracias.*"

"Got any cheese?"

"Why do you ask now?"

I shrug. I'm done.

"No cheese, Costello. I can give you some chilipiquin peppers to chew on."

I laugh and drink the coffee. Joshua mops the last beans with a piece of tortilla.

"I want to leave tomorrow," I tell him. I think tomorrow's Sunday.

"Sure."

"Let's go straight to Tridente. Over the mountains."

He nods. "Vicente's horses are trained. He wants us to shoot a stallion on our way out."

"Yeah?"

"Long yearling. Raiding the stock."

"Making the old heads look bad."

Joshua comes as close to smiling as he can usually get. Don Vicente Renova don't want us to shoot any stallion, just take him along. Must be a prize: Don Vicente don't want one of his stallions to kill the upstart and, more, don't want color mixing in the manadas. Each Renova stallion has a harem of mares matched to his color, and they all breed true.

"Blazing red chestnut," says Joshua. "Black points, linebacked. No brand."

I drink my coffee a minute. "You figure the Rangers are any thicker in the Bend?"

He lights another shuck. Mercedes clears our plates and I watch the shuck eat toward Joshua's work-stained fingers.

"Rangers, bounty hunters. Texas is getting crowded." He says it in that same way he says everything: voice like a blackrock cave, to match his eyes.

"Fences were a bitch this year, blocking the trail all through the plains. Damn shame, seeing the prairie wired like that. Hey, Mercedes, damn shame, right?"

"*Hables español,* Costello." Comes out testy.

"I got some cigarros, Chiso. You want one? Sure as hell beat them shucks."

He goes on smoking. Seems like he watches Mercedes, but I think he's looking at nothing. Then I hear Mercedes flip the curtain aside and go to the back room. Joshua and I smoke awhile in silence, until I decide I better follow Mercedes: what the hell.

She sits behind the back room on a boulder, sits in the hot sun with the rebozo still across her shoulders, but not sweating any more than any of us ever do. The sun hits her full in the face, and in her brown skin are lines, mostly around her mouth, smile lines and frown lines. She don't look at me nor squint at the sun neither, and her hair hangs over her shoulders in the black-red way it gets outdoors.

I put one foot on the boulder and my elbow on my knee and the cigarro between my middle finger and thumb. I take a drag and blow it out, away from Mercedes.

"You know I have to ride, Bella."

"Already I have told you that, Costello." She keeps staring straight ahead.

"I always have to leave. The drive is over, I have spent a month with you. I cannot stay here."

"*Claro.*"

"We have to go after a stallion, could take days, probably head west. Probably be halfway to Tridente by the time we catch him."

"*De acuerdo.* Do you hear me argue?"

I laugh, sounds harsh. Hell.

"Something amuses you, Costello?"

I feel my jaw twitch. Enough of the cigarro; stand up straight and grind it to tobacco crumbs against the gravel and turn to go.

But Mercedes stops me. "You leave, you leave," she says. "You stay, you stay. It is up to you, not me. Do you think I have nothing to do while you are off in your beloved Texas? Ha! I have all of Don Vicente's corrida, then. You think about it a moment, Costello. You are not here all that much, and I have to earn a living when you are gone. I do not ask that you support me with your wages, because it pleases me to be with you. But do not let yourself be fooled into believing you are the only one. *Comprendes?*"

"I would have it no other way," I say, knowing I can leave now and come back next spring and she'll be here waiting. "Remember, I have another life also."

We hold each other's eyes a long time, then I head back inside. "Let's get after that horse," I tell Joshua. "Today."

TWO

We come up a rise and Don Vicente's prairie sweeps around us in all directions. Can't see the hacienda from here, only the top of San Fernando's monastery ten or twelve miles south. This is north Coahila, and Don Vicente owns all of it between the Rio Grande to the east and the Sierra del Carmen way to the west. Only desert farther north, and other big haciendas south; God knows how many millions of acres Don Vicente Renova could work if he wanted to.

Mostly open spaces roll along between thickets of mesquite and cactus. Horses and cattle live on curly mesquite grass and browse the thickets for huajilla leaves and such, but most of the thickets here can't match those between the Rio Grande and the Nueces or in Refugio County for fierceness and protection, so except for outlaw cattle the stock stays on the prairie. The horses are half domestic, though they'll go back wild any time. From this rise we see their one-color manadas, each bunch apart from the next, dotted over the hills. The rainy season has just passed so the grass is only starting to go brown again though it's still mostly green. Looks like someone took a handful of jewels, each jewel a band of horses, and tossed it onto a green cloth so it stuck there, then fluttered the cloth in the wind to ripple hills and valleys across it.

"He's gone west," I say.

"Yup."

We turn our mounts into the sun and head west. Joshua said he saw the blazing red near here, but there are more manadas to the west, wilder ones with some ladina mares. Those stallions have to be tougher and meaner to steal the outlaw mares from the wild stallions that come onto the range now and again for better grass. If this red is headed that way with blood in his eye he'll have a hard time: any one of those stallions could skin him alive and wear his pelt to the dance spree after.

The ground rises easy here. We see peaks in the distance, the first ridge sharp and dark green, like a low breaking wave, then a second ridge behind it, higher, paler, same kind of jagged, then the big ridge behind that, color of smoke, bare above the pines, but we can't see the pines from here as it's near eighty miles off.

Grass mats under our horses' hooves, string of six geldings and two laden mules stretches out behind us. Tough trip crossing those mountains, and I figure we may have to shoot the red if he won't go. He might not go. I want him to go, and I never even seen him. I know him already, though. Know him well.

Sun's a bitch in our eyes. We could've stayed another day, set off earlier tomorrow.

"Wanna stop, Chiso?"

"Nope."

Me neither. We go on. Make about fifteen miles and hit a thicket running a good ten miles north and south. Big son of a bitch. We cut through: it's long going north-south, following a dry streambed, curving southeast at the bottom, but we're headed west and it oughtn't to be so thick. We go slow, never over a trot. Thorns are a bitch, too, but the stock's used to them and so are we. We put on waist-length ducking jackets and it's hot as hell with the mesquite and black chaparral holding down the little bit of moisture from that disappeared stream. I could use some water, so I take a draw on one of my canteens. Wrong one: rum from Don Vicente's, going sour in the heat. I dump it.

We dodge catclaw and huisache, watch for signs of horses, wild bulls, rattlesnakes. I seen enough rattlers for one day before I even woke up. We can hear them as we pass, rattling under the prickly pear, or maybe it's the brush breaking: noisy in the brush, pops as you go by. Can't creep up on man or beast out here, good place to lay low if you can stand it.

Ahead twenty yards it opens. Black chaparral is dark evergreen and it's like riding through a forest of thorns. You can see where it's clearer ahead. We near the edge and Joshua stops. I hear it too: screaming. Not human, not even animal. Screaming like a man burned alive. Then silence.

Then the stock gets fidgety in the brush.

"Tie them off," says Joshua in front of me. I do. We ride to the edge of the thicket. We can hear the thudding against the earth before we get there, we're trying to keep so quiet even with the brush all around. We're downwind, too. We can hear them whistle and nicker: they're taking a break, rallying for the next round. They whistle shrilly, bore holes in your ears.

We ride to the edge of where the open prairie rolls toward the first ridge of mountains far off and the prairie is green, dotted with mesquite, open, unfenced. The mares bunch near the thicket, shifting nervously but silent. The stallions circle each other, tails out, nostrils flared, breath coming so fast and rough you can hear it: huh-huh-huh-huh.

The old one is black and his manada is mixed: wild herd and wild leader. Ladinos, cimarrones. The blazing red chestnut plucks his legs high off the turf with each step.

"Arabian," I murmur.

Joshua nods.

But he's mustang, too, pure mustang. The Arabian blood comes from the depths of his line, he just brought it all back and he's magnificent for it. Muscle moves like waves under his blood-red coat. He shines in the sun, he glistens. He arches his neck, holds his head like a highborn prince; he has that slight dip between wide-set eyes, small muzzle, arrow-pointed ears. His black mane hangs long over his neck and his tail, though set high, pretty near touches the ground; black rings his eyes and ears and runs in a stripe down his back. Pure Arabian, pure mustang.

He charges first. Rears and strides in, front hooves slashing, lips back off white teeth that can shred a hide, ears flat against his head like a panther's. The black rises to meet him, nearly jumps on both hind legs, both almost off the turf at once. A black foreleg snakes, a red whips from the side, sinks into a black shoulder: thud, crack. The black backs off. The red follows, screaming. The black rises again higher and he's near as tall as the mountains behind, he bluffed before, he's bigger than the red and stronger. They're both wild, you can see it in their eyes, white all around when they scream and charge: they never blink, never close, even when those hooves strike to the bone.

The red slashes close with his teeth, under the black's head and around to his neck, rakes flesh off the neck. Blood spills over his muzzle. The black crashes hooves onto the red's back, the red's legs start to buckle and he backs and you can see he's winded and hurt but he don't give up for a second. He prances off, head high, blows through delicate flared nostrils that I expect to see blood come out of any minute with the snorting moisture.

The black whistles. The red tosses his mane back and forth across his neck, shock of black over his wide forehead, trots off and turns slowly, slowly, you'd think he's retreating but he's circling. The black whistles, stands with taut muscles rippling under his hide.

Bright blood streams over his neck, white foam covers his withers. The red trots farther off, circles slowly, slowly.

The black whistles.

The red spins on one hind hoof, charges, ears go flat, lips disappear. He's all pounding legs and teeth, neck stuck out, he's a bullet from a gun. He hits the black and the black's front leg buckles sideways and he nearly falls. But then he spins on those front hooves, hind legs thrust into the red, sharp hooves smash into lathered sides, cave in that blazing red chestnut hide, crunch the ribs underneath.

The red starts to go down.

"He'll kill him."

Joshua nods and shortens his horse's reins and the horse tosses its head; mine does too. I shift my rope, touch it to make sure it's there.

The red goes down. The black rears, hooves climb the sky. He screams.

A rider flies out of the thicket and spurs toward them.

"What the hell—"

Joshua looks.

Our mounts strain to go. We hold them.

The red rolls and the black's hooves hit the earth hard enough to loose the grass. The black rears. The red gets his front feet under him.

"Yaaaa!" screams the rider.

Jesus Christ, it's a girl.

I glance at Joshua and his straight harsh lips part and the black-rock caves of his eyes open for a second, the light gets in, lights as much as it ever will. I never seen him light up like that. Ain't happy or surprised or nothing, just lit up. Then dark as ever, but he keeps watching her.

She rides a huge gray with long fine legs, looks over sixteen hands and near thoroughbred, though no pure thoroughbred could survive out here. No saddle, just the bridle and bit, and that horse runs flat out, hell-bent-for-leather, faster than I ever seen any horse run.

The black wheels and takes one gander at that gray and the girl and races to his mares, races around and around them biting, screaming at them to get the hell out of here, tears chunks from their poor startled hides.

The red lunges to his feet, plants himself, and faces that girl head on. Hell if she don't screech to turn a thousand charging Comanches. Her hat flies off and flaps from a rawhide thong against her back. Wind plasters her leggins against her legs and shirt against her body while her jacket flies behind like a waist-length cape. She has short chestnut-color hair blown off a tanned face, and that's near all I can tell she moves so fast.

The red stands his ground and the gray and the girl charge him like they'll bowl him right over. The gray has at least a hand on him and plenty of weight, the red's quicker on his feet but wore out from fighting.

"Yaaaa!" the girl screams, near on top of him now.

The red snorts and wheels and takes off for the hills. Runs flat out.

"He's as fast as the gray."

"Yup."

The girl and the horses never look back.

"Come on!" I holler. We spur.

The red gives that girl a hell of a race, but two miles out he wearies. We stay a quarter mile behind.

"She's got no rope," I say.

"Little one."

"No lariat."

Joshua watches her. He knows what she'll do. So do I, but I can't believe it. But she does it: draws alongside that wild, blazing red chestnut stallion who just finished showing he could near skin another horse bigger and older, and here this girl glides from her gray onto his back, grabs his sides with her knees and his mane with one hand, throws that little hair rope over his neck and then a double half hitch round his nose to make a bosal, and she rides him like God rides the thunderheads.

THREE

We figure to let the girl wrestle with trailing that wild red stallion through the Sierra del Carmen, so we stay a good ten miles back the whole way across northern Coahila, sometimes more on account of scarce water. Five days pass and we ought to make the border tomorrow, depending what the girl does. Hills are rough and parched here, even after last month's rains, so we make a dry camp. Next day we set off again.

The girl picks up speed, looks like she moves at a fast gallop, probably to get through Rurales territory.

Joshua stays at a lope with our stock while I light out after the girl. Four hours later I ride into a dry canyon with high red ridges on either side capped by boulders and brush that stand out black against the sky. Creosote speckles the ground on the canyon floor, gives that faint familiar odor you can smell all over the desert of the Big Bend. River ain't far off; my horse can smell it and I can sort of feel the moisture in the air.

I got no love for riding into the sun like this, can't see a damn thing and the country's full of bandits and lawmen both. I yank my hat low for shade, but it does no good when I search the bluffs. Great way to get shot. I pull the Winchester from its boot and lay it across my lap.

Three miles farther and the girl's voice bounces off the canyon walls, husky and strong and you got no idea which way it come from.

"*Parate*!" It means halt.

I pull up, look all around. Nothing to see but red walls, creosote, ocotillo and every other kind of cactus, no girl.

"Drop your guns!" Still can't tell where she is. Sounds like everywhere.

A rifle shot cracks off the walls. Bullet kicks red rock and flushes a quail from a bush to my right. So she's up front with the sun directly behind her. My horse dances. I take off my flat-crowned hat and wipe my forehead with my sleeve, put my hat back on and lean on the saddle horn.

"Hot in the sun," I shout. "Whyn't y'all come out so we can find some shade?"

I see her then. She climbs down the bluff nimble as a mountain sheep, holding that rifle pointed loosely in my direction. She wears a man's clothes, or a boy's, seeing as she's not over five feet tall. Beat-up brown hat, loose-tied red bandana, faded green collarless cotton shirt open at the neck, longjohns under that; leather leggins and woolen breeches. Boots, high-heeled with what might be tarnished silver spurs.

"I like them spurs," I say.

She keeps climbing down.

She packs as much artillery as I do: Colt, old Spencer, probably a slew of knives and other tools of the trade.

She stops twenty feet from me, holds that Spencer in one hand by the stock so she can raise and fire easy, and I know she would've hit me before if she wanted. Which is why I kept my guns.

She has green eyes tending toward brown like the prairie is now; kind of a round face with a kid's pug nose and not much of a mouth; freckles. Short chestnut hair straight and lank, tucked behind her small ears, which stick out. She has the littlest hands I've ever seen, and all of her except the small breasts looks like anybody's kid brother. I figure she's going on eighteen.

"You sure got a nasty way of looking at a person," she says in that husky young voice. "Who the hell are ya?"

I laugh. "I'm offering a million-dollar reward and a shot of tarantula juice to the first one can answer that."

"You a bounty hunter?"

"Nope."

"Cattle detective?"

"Nope."

"Mighty scruffy for a Ranger."

"Mighty on the wrong side of the Rio, too."

She glances toward the bluff, where I figure she tied the horses.

"Now you're getting on to me," I say.

"Them horses is mine."

"The gray."

"Both."

"You're a common horse thief, sweetheart. That red is mine."

She shifts and slings the rifle onto her shoulder. I can see she's ready to deal. "I got grub," she says, "if you're innerested."

I touch the brim of my hat. "See you for supper, Bellaca."

She touches the brim of hers. "Right, Costello."

Bellaca, which means rogue, is a rustler and a thief, and I figured that's who this girl had to be though I never seen her before.

At dusk we three set around a mesquite fire longside the Rio Grande in the Big Bend's Boquillas Canyon. We'll cross upriver from here tomorrow, near San Vicente but not too close on account of the law or bandits or whoever else might be hanging around. Boquillas is safer for tonight.

Joshua ain't took his eyes off Bellaca since we got here, watches her from that blackrock cave of his. She don't pay it no mind, or seems not to. Joshua can set anyone to worrying with that stare, studying so quiet-like, never a word except a nod and a " 'Bliged" on first meeting. Puts some folks off.

Bellaca munches a charred twist of meat from the goat she stole. I can't stand goat, so I shovel in beans we brought on one of the mules and wish for a drink of more than Rio water, still so muddy you have to strain it through the bandana, even a month after the rain. Hardly any rain this year.

Bellaca says, "So you wanna buy that stallion."

I laugh through the beans. "Buy him with a rope."

"Ain't no one stringing me up, Costello. I catched that red fair and square."

"Sure, off Don Vicente's range."

"You work for the old grandee, huh? I knew that, seen you over there trailing out them big herds. Trail boss, hell. Pete Jackson, trail boss. He know who you really are?"

"Better'n I do, sweetheart. Better'n you, too."

She gnaws at the bone a minute and I rein in my temper. I don't need shit from some pug-nosed cow thief.

"I know all about you," she says finally, wiping the words on her sleeve. "Chiso, too. You know who I am, so I know who you are. I just know a little more."

"Bellaca the Rogue. Rustler, thief, slippery as a river eel to the Rurales, figured for a boy on some fliers, real name, let's see Chiso, real name—"

"Alice Kimberly," he says.

"Kim," she says, pronto.

"Alice," I say, grinning.

She tosses the bone at me and smiles, and the smile takes the edge off real nice.

"Kim," I say.

"Get up to Ogallala this year?"

"I'm surprised you don't know."

"Pass me some of that water."

I hand it to her. Joshua still watches her in his quiet way, and she still pays no mind. I like her for that and bet he does too.

"I went through Ogallala in August. Sure beats Dodge."

"Too much law in Dodge. I got up this year too, signed on with a drive outta Live Oak County, clear to the Blackfoot Agency. Best cow year I seen. All backed up south of the Red at Doan's, more'n the biggest buffalo herd ever. I clumb up a knoll for a looksee and you got cows clear back to Monterrey, seems like, all bunched long that river. You stuck in that?"

"We crossed before they ran. Heard it was bad."

She laughs: throaty, husky, head back. "Took us near ten days to untangle those brutes after they stompeded, like a regular roundup. We made like back in the diamond, split them up and started over. Too bad you missed it."

"No, it ain't."

"No, it ain't at that."

"Listen, they know you was a girl?"

"Not at first. Later, sure. They didn't care much, after I set them straight. I got no parts their mamas ain't got, and they got nothing new to me, so what's the difference? I can sing the Texas Lullabye sweet as any feller."

"I reckon. Who was the boss?"

"Moseby Sanders. I think he savvied me all along, figured to play a joke on the hands. Worked, too. Rumor got started and they's all whispering amongst themselves, one to the next like a bunch of old hens over a bad-colored egg. Finally I up and asks what's all the talk and one of the boys—I think he lost drawing straws—he comes out and says he got to ask if maybe I'm a little different from the rest. 'Different?' I says. 'Different how?' I'm all innocence, you know. 'Well,' says he, red as a whore's petticoat, 'Well, we all wondered if y'all might be a girl.' Blurted it right out like that, once he got going.

"I took to laughing so hard my sides near split, and soon they's all laughing, too, figuring I'm a boy same as they are and they're all so relieved they just got to laugh. I take a gander over at old Mose, who's hunkered by the fire with his whiskers about buried in his steak, hiding his face so the boys won't see he savvied me all along.

"Then I says to these hands, ''Scuse me, boys, but I gotta go behind the wagon a minute.' I walk back a ways and squat, and one by one the boys' heads pop round the side of the wagon, and when they see me squatting they like to jump on their horses and stompede clear back to Live Oak County."

I'd take on a whole tribe of Comanches for some whiskey right now. Somehow yarns without a bottle don't go down as well.

"You ought to seen those boys," Kim says.

"I reckon."

"Listen, you wanna buy that horse? You owe me after letting me drag him cross those mountains alone."

I chuckle. Joshua gets out the makings and rolls a shuck. I pull a cigarro from my vest and light it.

"Want it?" I ask the girl.

She takes it and I light another.

"Told you, we ain't buying that horse, he's already ours. Come off Don Vicente's range, Renova horse."

"You see a brand on him?"

"Yeah, right."

"I catched him. He's mine to sell. You don't wanna pay the price, he's still mine. You do, he's yours. I never stole a horse in my life."

"I don't believe that."

She gets her back up some, I can tell. So all right, she never stole a horse. Not this one, either. I figure we trailed him and she caught him, so I can pay half. No more.

"Half."

She laughs. "Like hell. These Don Vicente's cigarros? Right tasty."

"Half, no more."

"Half of two hundred is one hundred."

"You count better than you savvy horses. Two hundred for a ladino yearling! Oughtta string you up for the idea. Listen, that's some gray you got. How much thoroughbred's he have in him?"

"Most. And he ain't for sale."

"Don't he give you trouble in the brush?"

"Don't run him in the brush."

"You come out of that thicket on him."

"Thicket ain't fifty feet wide where we come out."

"Reckon you know that country right well."

"Reckon that's why Don Vicente moved his cows off it, do you?"

I smile. "Reckon."

We set around smoking awhile, watching the stars come out and the moon rise over the mountains and listening to the birds and evening rustlings in the desert brush along the river, which laps by flat and brown and slow going into the canyon.

Kim gets to her feet and walks from the firelight into the night. I follow her. The horses, hobbled, stand quiet except the red, who tosses his head, flips that black mane. Kim has him on a cabestro beside the hobble, with the knot buried deep. Can't no horse pull up a knot buried proper, because he'll pull back when he has to pull up to get it out. He ain't going nowhere. Kim makes to pat him but he snorts and bares his teeth. Smells good near the horses, cool now with the sun sunk and the moisture coming off their coats. It's a thick smell, goes deep inside your senses and makes you feel like nothing can hurt you with a fast horse near at hand.

Kim walks toward the river and I follow her.

"Try anything and I'll break your shooting arm," she says. "The way the stories go, droving ain't all you do."

"I shoot with the other hand too."

Behind us Joshua laughs. I'll be damned.

We get to the river bank and Kim stops. The moon, on the near side of full, sends bits of light off the water, and across the river the Chisos loom big and black against the stars. It's a hell of a nice night.

"Almost as light as day out here," I say.

"Some days, I reckon."

I keep quiet for a minute. Then: "I never seen anyone get on a horse like that."

She shrugs. "Been doing it for years. Nothing to it once you learn how, no more'n holding a stompede."

"That ain't so easy."

"You ever ride out front of one, singing?"

"Best way to stop them."

The moonlight catches her smile. I brush her cheek lightly with my fingers. Her skin is smooth and has the finest layer of downlike hair near her ear. She turns her head away and I drop my hand. Then I chuckle.

"Why do you laugh?"

"Dunno, just feel like it, I guess. Ain't laughing at you."

"You always do what you feel like?"

"Mostly. Why not? Plenty I want to do and likely not a whole lot of time to do it in. So I do what I feel like and it has to be good enough. Sometimes it ain't, but I don't think about that."

"Never?" She touches my arm but pulls her hand away pretty quick. Somewhere toward Mariscal Canyon a wren calls, its song sweet as a kiss, and we turn to go.

Back at camp Kim turns in and I set at the fire with Joshua, both of us smoking. After awhile I notice he's looking at my left hand, studying it real careful-like. He's been awful strange today, specially tonight.

"You all right?" I ask.

He draws on the shuck. I can't figure this bit with the hand, until finally he up and says, "As I recollect, you can't even shovel shit with that left hand. But maybe my memory's getting soft." And that's about the longest piece I've ever heard him say.

FOUR

Next day we trail toward Glenn Springs and Juniper Canyon beyond. River water drips off our leggins before the sun burns the last of it.

The Chisos rear in front of us, a wall of rock a mile high, safe for renegade Indians and outlaws and folks that savvy both, but no one else. Desert surrounds the mountains, deep sands in places, rocks on shallow sands mostly. Creosote puts out that aroma everywhere, and here and there an ocotillo thrusts a stalk with a red arrow at the end. A roadrunner paces across our path, swerves west past saw-needled lechugilla and ropy fine-thorned cholla. In places the cactus grows so thick and thorny it seems to wrestle with itself. Prickly pear spreads fat bristled leaves everywhere, sometimes tall as a man, usually low and twisted, thrusting for your ankles. Got to watch the prickly pear flats: rattlers lie up there in the daytime.

Ain't so hot as in San Fernando, but drier. Fall is one of the best times here, or maybe I like coming back after eight months gone. Still, I got no more love for these cactus and the Big Bend *gente* than for anywhere else. Juniper is nice but Juniper never seems real, more like a dream, and when you wake up you grieve for it. Sure Juniper's nice, if the springs run and September brings rain and the prickly pear don't shrivel. No rain and it can shrivel to hard gray-green wrinkles and the stock have no way to drink: no springs on the hillsides, no rain in the draws, no cactus, and the Rio gone to stinking mud. Then Juniper is hell and the stock starts dying off, and you know the dream left you for someone else's land of nod.

So we ride along the sandy rise that leads to Glenn Springs and Robbers Roost, where other small ranchers run what I figure from the brands is Mexican wet stock. The Chisos slope down to meet us on either side by midmorning, and I know we're into the lower end of Tridente by the scrubby juniper trees that dot the mountainsides and mark the beginning of Juniper Canyon.

Tridente is called Tridente because of three holes high on the walls above it: they look like someone took a pitchfork, a giant pitchfork, to the rock and gouged three caves. There's a black burned spot above the middle one.

You could call Tridente a ranch, but really it's a log cabin at the back of the canyon, under the South Rim of the Chisos, under the three caves, with some cow and horse stock living there because the water's as good as anywhere west of the Pecos and the mountains hold back the wet northers. You can't see the cabin until within a hundred yards, within rifle range; it sets behind a small hill on one side of the canyon.

As we ride near in the late morning, stones that crunch under the horses' and mules' hooves give way to gamma grass. That red stallion prances sideways like he's found his long-lost home and just itches to give it a run-through. He has spirit, that red, and when he rolls his eyes the black around them rims the whites and makes him look wilder than a snaky longhorn. And snaky longhorns are the wildest critters God ever put in a South Texas thicket, meaning the wildest anywhere.

We still ain't resolved the question of who owns that horse, though each of us thinks it was resolved way back, we just can't agree on how. I'd pay fifty or even seventy-five, but that's for me to know and Kim to find out.

Andy grazes the stock on the sides of the canyon: Juniper ain't steep-sided like a lot of canyons, but slopes up gradual on three sides. At the mouth it fans out, and as you leave the gamma grass goes to coarse chino, the sage pales, then even the chino grass thins and it's rocks and sand, back to the desert and on to the Rio. Good thing we're coming and not going. Stock grazes real contented, never even looks up as we three and our horses and mules and that prancing red stallion pass through.

We ride round the little hill and Andy waits in the doorway to the cabin, got his half arm raised to the doorframe and leaning on it, rawhide door flap open behind him, and his only hand on his hip and a big grin on his black Negro face. Andy lost the lower half of his right arm in a dispute over some money. He and Joshua and two other pards, Ryan Buckley and a first-class bastard name of Sheriff, was robbing a bank, they got the money but Andy lost his arm. Folks say a Colt's slug can kill you, but buckshot at close range can cut you in half and leave you screaming; sometimes you get lucky and all it cuts in half is your arm.

Andy has a wife up Panhandle way, Rafaela. Married her back near New Orleans, in the seventies, moved to Texas with Rafaela and the Sutherlands. Rafaela's mama was a Sutherland slave, some say Rafaela's a daughter to old man Garth Sutherland. I ain't much on Negro blood, understand, for myself I mean, but that Rafaela's a beauty if I ever seen one: carries herself just so, chin tilted up, sly smile, and a way of holding her pine-color eyes half-closed so she watches you out from under dark lashes.

Andy has the darkest skin of any of his race, so dark it looks kind of rough or even blue, no shine to it, rough like charcoal. He has a wide-nostriled nose and blue-black lips and forehead inclining toward hair he shaves so short sometimes he looks bald. He's shorter'n me, stocky built, hitches his old woolen trousers up with suspenders over a yellowed undershirt. Never wears no hat or jacket or leggins, even for brush work or cold weather. Never wears boots or spurs, only moccasins. Makes the best rawhide ropes in West Texas, sells them through Ignatz Kleinman's general store in Presidio, though only Kleinman knows Andy makes them and he never lets on to the customers though they ask plenty, since Andy's wanted.

Andy has a way of looking at you like you amuse him, like he just played a joke on you only you don't know it yet. Tilts his head to the side and looks at you that way, got big dark eyes and you just know his close-shaved head has stored up everything a Negro man's ever seen a white man do; he's seen it all, I reckon, been hurt by it, too, only instead of crawling he looks at you like the joke's on you. Pisses a lot of white folks off, maybe enough to account for why he lost half an arm in the bank job and no one else got a scratch. Maybe. I never knew him with two arms, so I don't know if he had the same look before or got it to make up for losing that arm. Anyway, he can still toss a rope and brand a cow, and rustle grub better'n anyone in the Bend. Rafaela's supposed to be ranch cook for the Sutherlands, and if she can fry doughnuts half as good as Andy I'm heading north.

Now he studies Kim, who gets off her gray racehorse. That blazing red chestnut stallion is necked to the gray; he nips at Kim's shoulder but she pays him no mind.

"Howdy," she says to Andy and sticks her hand toward him.

He smiles like usual, not grinning just smiling wisely, and he takes her right hand in his left and shakes it tight and says, "Hello, Bellaca," in his low voice that sounds like rich black soil looks. So he knows too. Hell, sometimes the border gets downright cozy.

"Kim," she says, and goes inside with Joshua and Andy while I take the horses to the little wood-fenced corral near the cabin. I fix morrals of corn for them but of course the red wants no part of that.

"Righto," I say and slap him on the neck. He nips my hand and I slap him again, not hard. "Whatever you want, blazing red chestnut stallion. Just remember we saved your life." The other horses munch their corn, grind it between their teeth while I rub their backs with handfuls of dry grass. The red stallion eyes them, tries to make like he ain't interested. I hold the bag in front of him. He rolls his eyes and tosses his mane. His shoulder ripples and he switches that black tail that nearly touches the ground.

"Righto," I say again. "Maybe you'll learn." Maybe not. I unload the mules and grain and rub them and lug my saddle and the leftover provisions to the cabin. Joshua already took his saddle in and Kim has none.

A wind kicks up before I go inside, you can hear it in the trees. That red stallion raises his head on the thick arched Arabian neck, flares his nostrils at the breeze, and for a second you can see the whites of his eyes against the black rims: ladino, that stallion. I take a cabestro off my saddle, throw a loop around the red's neck and tie him to a corral post, and he looks at me like I'm closing the last door to the jailhouse, but proud, not beat.

"Don't worry," I say, "I ain't throwed away the key."

I go back to the cabin, and walking off I hear him paw the ground.

FIVE

Andy rustles a fine dinner of fried steak and red peppers, biscuits and sweetened pumpkin, which someone must've brought back from No Man's Land. On the ranch in Refugio County we had mostly Negro cowhands, and I spent all kinds of time in the bunkhouse listening to them yarn and sing. Bunkhouse had that thick Negro smell along with a mix of odors from old boots and lighted tallow, rawhide, dried cow dung, and licorice from chaws. The hands would spin slave stories, ghost tales, mostly, until I was too scared to walk back to the main house. So I'd stay with the hands many a night, fall asleep curled on a piece of rawhide on the floor and smelling that thick Negro smell.

This cabin at Tridente smells like that bunkhouse, and it's so full of tack and ropes and artillery that you can hardly turn around. There are two bunks with rawhide stretched across wood frames; there are shelves high on all the walls, one offering a whole bar of bottles from Don Vicente's, though low on rum, and I wish that rum hadn't spoiled on our way back here; and others with coffee and Bull Durham, cans of beans and tomatoes, piloncillo, which is brown sugar from Mexico;

and there are pegs on all the walls, too, for the tack and artillery: two shotguns, one a sawed-off Remington-Whitmore twelve-gauge and the other an English-made Winchester; a .44 Colt model 1872 Joshua picked up in Mexico, Andy's Smith and Wesson Schofield .45, a Winchester .44 carbine, and my old Spencer rifle that I never use anymore. I have the Winchester '73 now, but I keep the Spencer.

The frying steak and biscuits plumping in tallow in the Dutch oven set my belly to growling. Autumn sun makes the two small windows shiny squares, but in here it's dim and smoky. Kim lifts Andy's old guitar off the floor where it leans against the wall and asks who plays.

"No one now," I say.

She strums a finger over the strings: Andy keeps it tuned.

"Pete does some," says Andy.

Kim looks at me kind of funny.

I fish in my saddlebags for Rafaela's letter and give it to Andy. Every year she leaves a letter at Doan's Store, up on the Red River, addressed to me but really for Andy. He wipes his hands on his trousers and takes the letter, looks at it a minute, looks at me, and goes outside. He knows I missed seeing her this year, got to the Crossing too early and had to pick up the letter on the way back; knows without me saying.

Kim sets cross-legged on the bear rug with the guitar and plucks the strings in a little tune I never heard. She gives me that funny look again and I can't figure those prairie green eyes sometimes. Then she sings, or not singing but making small notes with her voice, no words, hardly any tune.

An hour later we sit outside the cabin, against the front of it, shaded from the autumn afternoon sun: Joshua, me, Kim, Andy. I wash down charred beef and peppers and puffy biscuits with Don Vicente's bourbon, and Kim goes on about where she come from. Says her pa come from the South to Denver for some prospecting and her ma was a box rustler but some landlady everyone called the Madam raised her. Or something like that: I'm resting with the whiskey, holding the bottle by the neck next to my leg and half of the bourbon gone already: I ain't had a drink since San Fernando and damn if it don't slide down easy.

I look up the slope in front of us, juniper going darker into pinyon pines and Douglas fir and rock above that looks blasted with a sawed-off shotgun. Then sky as blue as the Gulf but flatter and no sharks. Used to set on the beach and pretend to see them black triangle fins coming at me, then Ma calling, "Peter Jack! Peter Jack!" Guess we never traveled to the beach much, only once or twice.

"You grew up in Colorado?" I say to Kim.

"Partly, why?"

"Worked a spell there. Maybe we met up."

She laughs. "When was you there?"

"Twelve years back. Seventy-two, that'd make it."

"You must've been pretty young. I was only six."

I take another long pull on the bourbon and look at the sharkless blue sky. "I was fourteen."

"What could you do at fourteen?"

"Everything wrong. How'd you wind up in Texas?"

"Oh, the Madam got tired of Denver and moved me and a couple of her girls to El Paso. Never wanted me following her trade, but weren't a whole lot else for a girl to do so I took to riding and shooting and learning cow. Linked up with a Mexican family and they taught me about mustanging."

"I like that red," says Andy.

"Nice, ain't he? Might even outrun my gray. We oughtta race them sometime."

I can't figure that I was in the same town with her. "How old were you when y'all moved to El Paso?"

"Chrissakes, Pete, I never knew you in Denver. You think I was innerested in cowhands at age six?"

I shrug. "Be something, wouldn't it? I mean, I never knew anyone in two places before."

"Want some pumpkin, Pete?" says Andy.

I take a mess of it, let the juice drip off and eat it nearly whole. Got piloncillo all over it, sweet as sin to a boy. After that I feel some drowsy, as much from resting as from riding and drink, and dreams like clouds roll in and over and break off into each other so I forget them as soon as they pass. Snatches of conversation stick together into pictures: someone says horse and the red stallion comes out of a cloud front toward my eyes, someone says hawk and he sprouts wings and flies over my head, someone says rain and he dissolves to drops, each a tiny horse splashing to the dust, turning into dust, gone in a devil of dust that settles and nothing left but baked plain.

"I'm gonna buy that horse," I say to myself.

I open one eye and Kim says, "One hundred."

"Yeah, right. You pay seventy for this meal and we got a deal."

She grins at Andy.

"Then it's my horse," he says.

"Sure," she says.

"Sure," I say.

"Horse ain't worth a hundred," says Joshua. "Fifty, maybe."

Kim don't say nothing.

I've got to have that horse. I close my eyes and there he is again. Sure beats snakes.

Kim and I hang our arms over the corral fence, lean on it from outside; Andy and the blazing red are inside. Joshua works stock off in the canyon. The red has no rope on him; Andy lays out the braided rawhide on the ground, big loop, and the red watches from across the corral, fifty feet off, flinching his hide like flies are after him. Andy works easy, makes like the red ain't even there, and you can see it gets under the red's skin: never takes his eyes off that rope or the man laying it out. I reckon he never seen or smelled a Negro and it's got him some nervous but curious too: he stretches his thick curved neck toward Andy.

Andy ties one end of the rope to a corral pole and hooks his moccasined toes under the hondo, all the while moving real casual like he don't know the red is there. Then he glances at me and Kim and kind of grins.

I take off hollering for the red, and he was so fixed on Andy I like to scare him out of that shiny hide. He jumps straight up and lands running.

Andy jerks his foot up sharp and that rope flies through the air. The red runs away from me, toward Andy, and that loop drops over his head as neat as you please. He swings around but don't stop for a minute, races out the full sixty feet of that rope. The rope jerks shut around his neck, stretches a good four feet and yanks the red back on his haunches nearly flipping him over, and for the most Godawful instant of my whole life I think it will break his neck.

But the corral pole gives and then holds, and the well-greased rope gives more. Before we know it the red wheels and comes at Andy, ears back, teeth bared, and I swear I hear him snarl. Andy lights out, jumps clear over the fence and keeps running, and damn if that blazing red chestnut stallion don't fly over after him and he races, races, and Kim and I holler at the tops of our lungs, scared but laughing through it. Andy runs so God damn fast, I never seen anyone go like that.

The rope pulls tight again, throws the red nearly to the ground but he stays on his feet, quivers all over. He screams, and it licks at the juniper and the pines and my ears and soul like flame.

Andy swings a wide berth around that ladino red stallion, walks to us blowing hard and shaking his head.

"You give her fifty for that horse and you're paying for your own broke back," he tells me.

"One hundred," says Kim.

"Seventy-five."

"Sold."

She looks into me with her prairie green eyes, and for a minute I think she would've given him to me for free. Hell, probably as much to see me get throwed as for any other reason. I hold out my hand and she takes it and we shake, and we hold on longer than it takes to sell a horse. Then I give her a quick kiss on the cheek, she lets go and backs off but she looks toward Andy, not me, and when she sees he's watching the horse and not us she stops backing off. I just smile at her and damn if she don't get a red tint under them freckles. Damn if she don't.

So now I got to figure a way to bring that horse in and ride him and I don't particularly care to do it with everyone watching. Truth is I ain't sure he can be rid beyond the kind of wild run Kim had on him that first day. He's mighty young, too, but better along than most yearlings, probably not a month shy of two. I figure to do this slow, real slow, with plenty of piloncillo.

No help for Andy and Kim watching, what the hell. I sling a hackamore over my shoulder and work along the rope toward the horse, who tugs the end of it, rolling his eyes and tossing his mane. Five feet from him I fish some piloncillo from my vest pocket.

"Hey, *caballo,* you want some sugar? Sugar, hey?" I talk low to him. He snorts and tosses that fine red head with the black eyes and muzzle. I turn the lump of brown sugar between my fingers and thumb. The red stretches his neck toward it, pulls back, prances. He ought to be pretty hungry; ain't allowed anyone near enough to grain him. But he don't act hungry, just proud.

"Piloncillo, hey? Maybe you like Spanish. *Habla usted español, ladino?*"

He nickers kind of low, stretches his neck again, smacks his lips. I roll the sugar into my palm, open my hand flat and hold it under his nose. He smacks his lips.

"Hey, *caballo,*" I say.

He eats the sugar, his muzzle bristles against my palm. I let the hackamore drop from my shoulder into my hand and slide it over his head before he's done munching. He tosses, but too late. I pull down on the reins. He rolls his eyes. I grab the sides of the bridle, hold his head still, breathe into his nose. He tries to back off, but the rawhide rope is already stretched so taut you could walk on it.

With my hands I pat and stroke all over his face and neck and body, down his legs, over his back. I put more pressure on his back, press with both hands. This goes on for a good half hour, and all the while I'm hoping Andy and Kim get bored and move along, but they perch on the corral fence watching, and now Joshua watches too.

I lead the red toward the corral. He jerks back, throws his head up but follows me in. I hook a short rope to the bridle, slip the long one off his neck and tie him to a corral pole. Then I take my saddle blanket from over the corral fence and rub it along his back. He dances sideways, rolls his eyes. I keep on with the blanket until he quiets down.

"Ain't you three got nothing better to do?" I say to my audience in the same low voice I use for the horse. They all shake their heads as though this horse and my soon to be sore butt are all that matter on earth. Joshua pushes his hat back on his head, folds his arms along the corral fence and rests his chin on them.

The blazing red gets used to the blanket after a spell, so I heft the saddle and hold it near him. He takes one look and up goes his back and off flies the blanket. He comes back to earth and stares at me. I could swear he laughs inside, but that's a good sign. I retrieve the blanket and go through that part again. Finally I set the saddle on him and just as he takes off straight up I cinch it tight. The stirrups are tied so they don't flap, but hell if it matters, the way he bucks he'll flap them loose.

I try to talk to him but he don't listen. He prances and bucks and rears against the halter rope. I glance over my shoulder. Kim covers her eyes but grins. Andy shakes his head and Joshua goes inside.

"Y'all enjoy the show," I tell Andy and Kim and then I go inside too: that horse has a lot of buck left before I get on.

"Think he can be rid?"

Joshua rolls a shuck and lights it. "Dunno."

"I ain't going to break him down. Ain't gonna castrate him neither. He can't be rid I'll let him go."

"He figures that out he'll never let you ride."

He figures that out and he will let me ride. That's what I believe, but I don't say so except to shrug.

"Paid seventy-five for him," I say.

Joshua nods slowly. "Good price."

After a couple of hours I head to the corral and my audience collects again. I blow in the horse's nostrils and talk to him low and pat him all over. Then I put my hands on the saddle and lean on my arms, and he stands it all so easy I'm afraid he's soft already. He ain't though: look at his eyes, the way he flares those fine nostrils, holds that tail, arches that neck.

"Y'all never had a man on top," I say. "Only a little girl mustanger, light as a feather, no saddle."

I unhitch the halter rope, swing into the saddle and let him go. He bolts with a thrust from those muscled haunches, bolts through the open gate and fifteen feet on the first stride, hits the turf and takes off. Behind us, far behind, I hear whoops from Kim and Andy, but I know Joshua feels it the most inside, know it because I do too.

We are gone, just like that. Flying, and the ground blurs. Bushes become streaks, trees swipes of green. Red races for the back of the canyon, around a hill, toward a bunch of longhorns, scares them. They take after us, we leave them behind. Red stretches out, he has the longest stride I ever seen on a mustang. He flings deep divots of grass behind us, races, races, and I grip with my thighs, knees, ankles, boots. I ain't coming off no matter what and he knows it: we run as one.

"Yaaaa!"

Red lays back his ears, digs into the earth. There's a green blur under and a blue blur above. Wind whips my face, whips wetness from my eyes and into my hair, tears my hat off and flaps it. Wind's roar mixes with pounding hoofbeats, deafening, stabs my ears. I add my voice to it, lean forward in the saddle and the wind skirts over my back and we run faster than fast, so fast life can't never catch up. So damn fast, pushing, pushing, pushing against the earth, straining to fly. Flying.

The back of the canyon rises in front of us. Red strides onto the mountainside, looses small avalanches with sharp front hooves, climbs halfway up at a run before I start thinking I have to pull him in or he'll kill himself. But I hate to do it, it's like killing him anyway. But I do, I pull back, I talk low and pull back until he stops, quivering, both of us quivering, three-quarters of the way up that mountainside.

You can see the whole world from here. Sun going down turns Mexico to mountains of fire. Red snorts and I pat his neck. He's white with lather. Cool air dries our sweat: damn if my hair ain't soaked.

We stay a long time, until the fire dies and the air takes on the cool moistness of evening that makes the horse and the brush and the evergreen smell so rich. Red don't move a muscle, just watches day pass into evening while his sides swell gently, breathing against my legs. When the sun has gone he tosses his head and starts walking down the mountain, then trots and soon lopes, and I swear I never told him to do any of it.

He drops back to a walk a half mile from the cabin. Dusk quiets the canyon, fades the brush and trees into each other. We pass through a pasture where the other horses graze. They seem to form from the dusk, or from the earth itself, like coming out of a fog, and we must look the same to them, a man and a horse born of earth, because as we approach they lift their heads from grazing and watch us, silent and knowing. Red walks proud with his head high on that thick arched neck, never looking right nor left, never taking notice of them horses, proud, so proud.

At the corral an extra morral of corn hangs from a post. Red sucks deeply of water from the trough, then takes the morral like he was born to it. I unsaddle him and rub the sweat off his back with dry grass and wait for him to finish graining. A nightingale sings and I lean against the fence to listen. Yellow light spills from the cabin windows and notes from the guitar drift on the still air. Red finishes and I go inside.

Kim stops plucking the strings and looks at me. Joshua and Andy look too, and for a moment the whole world is so silent I can hear the blood in my veins. I take a new bottle of bourbon and settle with a drink. No one asks. Andy goes on cooking supper. Kim picks at the guitar, half humming. The whiskey spreads inside me as I sit on the bear rug, leaning against the wall.

"He's still the same horse he was at sunrise," I say finally, and we all kind of smile.

Later on Kim and I take a walk, past where Red stands quietly in the corral, through a draw where the grass grows soft and deep. Moon rises full, a great hunk of palomino light bobbing from behind the Sierra del Carmen, dusting the landscape with pale gold.

"I like it here," Kim says as we walk. "Like it right well."

I put my arm across her shoulders. She stiffens, but only a little. We walk up the draw a ways until the cabin's yellow squares of light are no more than specks. I stop and turn to her and I want to kiss her powerful bad, but I'm afraid she'll run off. I touch her hair, short and straight, run my fingers through it. She tilts her head back, closes her eyes, but only for a second. I feel her hand on my side through my shirt, and the skittishness comes through her warm fingers. She takes her hand away, leaves a cool spot.

"I been thinking about that story you told," I say. "The one about the trail drive."

Her eyes search mine.

"Ain't no way those hands could've took you for a boy. I knew you was a girl soon as I saw you ride out of that thicket."

"Yeah?"

"Yeah."

I tilt her chin and kiss her and she kisses me though I can tell she's never been kissed a whole lot. I put both arms around her and hold tight and her small breasts press against me so I touch her there. But she won't have it and I ain't surprised, so I kiss her again and we just lie down close to each other on that cool thick grass and watch the stars pop out, one by one, like somebody pricking holes in the big blue sky.

"He's so fast," I say.

"I know."

So I roll on top and kiss her again. Kiss her and more, but only so much as she'll have. Only so much, but maybe it's enough.

SIX

Long about December we have the stray bull calves rounded up and castrated and ain't much doing at Tridente besides training horses, so Kim and Joshua and I light out for El Paso. Takes more than a week to get there, especially since we only brung one mount each—Red ain't near ready so I ride my gelding—and it's nigh unto Christmas by the time we get in. I figure there's a week yet before the holiday, but El Paso will use any excuse to celebrate long and hard.

We clean up and buy new clothes, and Joshua and I get shaved. Halfway into the afternoon we set to drinking beer, resting from the long ride. Even after that bath I feel like a puff of dust goes up when I sit down.

Kim looks around the saloon and frowns like she can't figure something important. Finally she says, "I know what it is."

I draw on my beer and Joshua lights one of his shucks.

"Well," says Kim, "ain't y'all gonna ask me what it is?"

"What what is?" I mumble into the foam on my beer.

"What it is that feels so funny. We're in the wrong town, that's what. This just ain't El Paso."

Joshua lowers his shuck and looks at her. I shake my head and wave to the barmaid for more. Kim leans forward on her elbows.

"Now I know the sign outside says this here's Uncle Ben Dowell's saloon and that just a block yonder is the Gem Saloon—that's where the Madam used to work, like I told you—but I'd lay money some cowboy on a drunk took all the signs from the real El Paso and tacked them up in this city."

I set down my mug and look hard at her. We're about the only ones in the saloon, which is roomy and swept and cool, waiting for night. Someone's strung a garland of evergreen over the picture behind the bar: picture shows a naked lady reclining, looks right comical with the garland.

"I reckon, Alice, that you're the one off on a drunk, or else you've gone plumb loco. What the hell are you talking about?"

"El Paso. This ain't El Paso. And I ain't Alice, thank you."

"Righto. Then what city is this?"

She sighs. "It just growed up, I guess. I mean, it's so big now, nothing like the old days."

I shrug. "The railroad might've brung some new buildings, but the feel is the same."

Joshua switches his gaze from Kim to me. "It ain't."

"Well, it seems the same to me. Just a little bigger, nothing more. So the banks've got more money in them. So what?"

"Got a whole new bank," says Joshua quietly.

"Yeah. State National."

"Fancy name," says Kim.

"Christ, you two! So the city grows up, what difference does that make? Might think we just walked into a prison, way y'all carry on. Ain't like it's civilized or nothing."

Kim's face brightens. "I heard where Dallas Stoudenmire got killed, so at least there ain't such a great marshal no more."

"Dallas Stoudenmire got killed two years ago, and Gillett's no slouch, if he's still the one. Where've you been?"

"I knew that," she says. "I was just trying to look on the bright side."

El Paso's pretty lively most of the time, but with a few drinks under her belt she's downright wild. We lay around at the Central Hotel until it gets good and dark and the sounds of night wake us. We eat supper at the hotel and head for the nearest party, keeping on the lookout for lawmen.

We stride into the saloon, ears steeled for the noise. The piano player pounds "Pop Goes the Weasel" over the shouts of the drinkers. The floor vibrates with stomping feet of dancing cowhands, bandits, girls in ruffled satin cut low and high; money clanks on every table. Folks gamble or argue or dance; all of them drink. Screams of "Keno!" and a wide mix of cuss words top the roar, and the scent of my first whiskey blots that of sweat and smoke as I pour it down my throat.

We order a second round at two bits each and join some cowhands in a low stakes game of blackjack. After a little while one of them satin-clad girls saunters to the table and takes orders for a third round, then a fourth, but seems we just got here. Stuff works right quick, so that soon only Joshua manages to win anything. Cool head, Chiso. Looks like he been drinking as much as any of us, but part of him never gets drunk. Same part as don't laugh or talk much.

I take a gander at my cards and figure a queen and a four could use some help. What the hell.

"Hit me."

Card flicks through the smoke and brings the total to twenty, and maybe I'll beat Joshua on this one. He nods for a third card, then a fourth and a fifth: Five Card Charlie. Kim takes a couple and so do the others. We all place our bets, little stuff. When it comes time to lay out the cards, naturally Joshua has twenty-one.

I laugh. Even Joshua smiles a little.

"Gotcha that time, you bastard," Kim says, slurred.

"You gonna let her call you that?" asks one of the cowboys.

"Hell yeah, probably true," I say.

"Ain't you Pete Jackson?" says another one.

"Jackson," I say. "Never heard of him." I feel that whiskey pretty well and better watch out. I grin at the hand.

"Seen you at Doan's." He thrusts out his hand. "How'd y'all get acrost that river so fast? We had a helluva mess."

"So I heard."

Dealer deals another hand and Joshua wins that one too. After awhile the cowboys run out of money and toss the deck across the table.

"You going up next year?" this cowboy asks me. He ain't much over eighteen, from the looks.

"I reckon."

He follows the others out and I feel some uncomfortable, so I drink and the feeling fades.

The next place ain't so grand but it's more crowded. We survey the throng for badges, careful now on account of that cowboy. Room sways, dances, or I sway. Kim hangs on my shoulder like she's ready to fall down. Probably is. Joshua disappears into the smoke, so I grab Kim and swing her around, trade her off to the other dancers and catch her again, and her hat bounces at her back and her short, straight hair flies out when she spins. Piano player here has a banjo player to help. Everyone starts singing some song I never heard before, but Kim and I join in anyway. Dancing wears off some of the liquor, so we order more before moving on.

We hit near every one of them twenty saloons, a bunch more than once, or that's how it seems. One has a brass band that plays "The Lakes of Killarney" at least five times in a row, so now it plays inside my head even over the mariachis at the next one. Each place blurs into the next and out into the street until I can't hardly tell if I'm outside or inside or anywhere else for that matter. Kim gets lost along the way, seems I search the rest of the night before finding her.

"Where the hell you been?" I yell at her, only it comes out awful funny.

She giggles and kisses me on the mouth. I grab her and kiss her back, and we're lying on the boardwalk though God knows when we fell over. People stagger by, some stop to peer at us before tripping off to the next bar. I close my eyes but that's a mistake so I pull Kim to her feet and lead her inside to dance off the dizziness.

The next morning all I want to do is throw up. I don't want to open my eyes, but figure I better make sure I'm in the hotel room. I am: lying on the floor with my hat turned over next to my head and still wearing my gunbelt and one boot. Other boot's across the room. Kim's curled up beside me, dead to the world and one arm covering her face. Joshua's sprawled on the bed.

I drag myself to my feet and look out the window. Noon, or near it, with sun hard on the eyes but no shadows. Street's littered with men sleeping it off; not much traffic, must be Sunday.

I pull on my other boot and stumble downstairs to the hotel cantina. A girl, probably a whore, sits on the bar swinging her feet. A few folks eat quietly, looking like how I feel.

"Hey, cowboy," this girl calls, "looks like y'all had a good time last night."

"Hog-killing," I mutter. "Got any biscuits?"

"Sure. Sit down. Want some beer with them?"

I shake my head and sit. She hops off the bar and I stare at the table, feeling more or less like shit. After a minute the girl brings a basket of sourdough biscuits and I manage a bite.

"Coffee's coming," says the girl. "We hadda brew a new pot."

After the first biscuit I feel some better. The girl still stands by my side, so I tell her to sit. A man at another table clunks down some change and leaves. The girl looks that way but don't move to clear the plates.

"I saw y'all come in last night," she says. "I's standing right by them stairs when you and that girl come tripping and slipping through the door singing at the top of yer lungs some song I never laid ears on. You made it to the stairs but sure as hell couldn't make it up."

"You took us up?"

She laughs shrill enough to hurt my already sore head. "Hell no! I hadda haul in two cowhands, neither in much better shape than y'all. I tell you, this here's one wild town. My name's Rosalie, by the way."

"Obliged, Rosalie."

She looks me over for a spell, then fetches the coffee.

"You look kinda familiar," she says, pouring. "Been in these parts before?"

"Now and then."

"So what're you called?"

"Depends who's calling." I smile. "And why. My name's Pete Jackson."

She thinks a minute. "Trail boss?"

"The same."

She likes that, you can tell. "Where'd y'all go last year? Far up or just Dodge? I been to Dodge once. Ogallala, too. You trail up that way?"

"Clear to the Dakotas."

"Gets cold up there."

"Not in summer it don't. Not too much."

"Well, I didn't mean summer. You know."

She seems real young, fifteen at the most, and I wonder what she's doing here and in this line of work, though I've seen plenty of little girl cats before and never been bothered by it. I drink some coffee, which is too fresh and smooth, and eat another biscuit. Rosalie looks at the half-empty basket and at me, then jumps up. She moves awful quick. A second later she hurries back with a jar of honey, and the two of us take to dunking the biscuits in it. Makes our hands and the table sticky but sure beats the biscuits dry. Then Rosalie jumps up again and hurries back to pour more coffee. After that she stays at my side with an arm across my shoulders. I ignore it until she starts playing with my hair.

"Ain't it a little early to start working?"

She laughs that shrill way. "Not if you're innerested."

"The way my belly feels? You gotta be kidding."

"I hope y'all don't make love with your belly, cowboy, but if you do I'd love to teach you the right way."

"I don't. How about you sit down, okay?"

She sits, pouting. She ain't altogether ugly, though her hair's stringy and dull and pimples dot her face. She's skinny, too.

"Got any more biscuits?"

"You already had five."

I throw her a look and she heads for the kitchen. I reach for a cigarro, but they're upstairs and I don't feel like going after them. Rosalie plunks another basket on the table, takes care of some other folks, sits to watch me eat. I could eat biscuits all day.

After awhile she says, "You sure talk a lot."

"What do you want me to say?"

"I dunno. How's the weather?"

"Warm."

"Is it sunny out?"

"Course it's sunny out. Door's right over there."

"Y'all in love with that little cowgirl?"

"What kind of question is that?"

"Like any other, I reckon."

"Well, I ain't."

"You get anything off her?"

"That ain't what I'd call your affair, sweetheart."

She sits back in the chair, a hint wary. Then she laughs awkward and shrill and asks about the Dakotas. I tell her they're right nice. She wants to know how folks up there compare to folks down here so I tell her they ain't as talkative.

Kim comes in then, looking puffy round the eyes and a mite pale.

"Morning," I say.

She nods and mutters something.

"Try some of these biscuits."

She pulls out a chair and sits, turns paler at the idea.

I chuckle. Rosalie eyes Kim.

"How about another basket of these?" I say to Rosalie. "Coffee too."

She sticks out her chin and stalks to the kitchen.

"Young ain't she?" says Kim.

"You're a great one to talk."

She scowls. "I ain't in no mood for your teasing, Pete."

"Righto, Alice. Guess three years and a few tussles with the Rurales can make a lot of difference."

"They can. Now why'd you have to order me that crap? I'll probably throw up after the first bite."

"No, you won't. Look what they done for me."

"You've never looked better."

Rosalie returns and thrusts a basket and a cafecito at Kim, then leaves. I touch one of the biscuits: stone cold.

"I think she likes you," says Kim.

"Seems that way, don't it. Joshua still asleep?"

"Naw, he's on the porch, just setting there with his feet up."

"Wonder where he disappeared to last night."

"Said he got in a poker game, then come back here. Don't seem too hung over."

"Never does, the bastard."

"Sure gambles good."

"You know it. I think he memorizes the cards. And he's got a perfect poker face. Beats me every time."

Kim sips the coffee and grimaces. "I'm surprised he likes the bars. Didn't figure him that way."

"Ain't that way. Don't like bars and don't care about winning. I figure he just does it cause there ain't much else to do."

"He ever say?"

"Nope."

"Huh."

"Rosalie knows who I am. Recognized my name."

"Rosalie? You know her name?"

"What else was I supposed to do waiting for you lie-a-beds? Take in the view?"

She scowls.

"Hell, she almost had me in bed with her, maybe for free. You saved the day."

"I think I saved her."

Long about the time our hangovers head west we start in again. Figure we hit every place worth hitting last night, so this time we'll hit them in reverse order. Well into the night I feel about as good as a man can feel, dancing and singing and losing money, and the world floats around me all colors smoking one into the next, up in a poof and poof there's Kim and poof there's a new saloon.

Somewhere along the line we roll down the street and a passle of boys race round the corner shooting and whooping and a whole pack of dogs yipping at their heels, and you oughtta see their horses fly. I swear all their feet come right off the ground and those boys riding got hats big as houses and voices bigger than thunder. Whooping they race up that street past us and the other folk, all the dust fogs us in so we hack and cough, and that's when I get the idea for what to do next.

So I grab Kim by the wrist or some part and hold the bottle of whiskey in my other hand and drag Kim toward where we last saw Joshua. Sounds like she says I'm locoed and pulls away, but I can't hardly tell her from the longhorn steer next town over. Hell, I better stop and make sure, so I do, just stop and peer at her real close, and yup it's Alice Bellaca Kimberly all right. I just got to kiss her so I do, but damn if she don't push me away.

"Y'all're loco," she says, but then she takes to fits of laughter and says, "Okay, what the hell let's do it."

I take a long pull on that bottle and next thing I know we find Joshua coming out of Doc Manning's saloon, and next thing after that, well, damn if me and Kim ain't standing guard while he picks the lock on the door.

We sneak in and it's black after the street. All we can hear of the big fandango outside are muffled shouts and piano music like rain on a tin roof far off, and now and then a shot. My eyes adjust and damn if I ain't inside a bank fixing to rob it, a small bank with two teller's windows and a table behind them along with the safe in the left-hand corner and Joshua kneeling in front of the safe. Now I feel a little less drunk.

"Light a match," says Joshua.

I try to and nearly burn my fingers. Joshua does it and something tells me he might be pissed, so I want to ask why the hell he went for the idea, but I don't. Kim squats by him and he listens to the safe while his fingers work the lock. I lean back against the teller's counter and watch, and it hits me how easy this is. Too easy. Those boys whooping up the street was having a heap more fun.

The match goes out but Joshua don't bother with another. Streetlight filters through barred windows so you can see the shiny metal of the safe and the dark forms of Joshua and Kim after your eyes adjust. I set the bottle of whiskey on the counter and light a cigarro; no trouble with the match this time.

"What're you doing?" Kim whispers.

"Smoking. And no need to whisper. Ain't a soul out there cares what we're doing."

"That's right," Joshua says, quiet and dark. Then he twists the handle and opens the door.

I let out a lungful of smoke and the faint light makes it muddy yellow.

Kim sticks her hands into the safe and swears about all the gold. She and Joshua start pulling out bag after bag and I stand watching them, smoking, and somewhere along the line I clench my left fist so tight it hurts.

"How much you want?" Joshua says, still quiet and dark. "No way we need all of this."

I pitch the cigarro to the floor and grind it out. "None."

They look around at me.

"None," I say again. "I don't want none of it."

"What the hell are you talking about?" Kim demands.

"The money: I want you to put it back in the safe like it was before you got it out and close the door and spin the knob."

Kim looks at Joshua. "He's kidding, ain't he?"

"Nope."

"Jesus Christ! I ain't going to all the trouble of breaking into this bank and then just walk out! We come here to rob us a bank, and we're gonna rob us a bank!"

"No we ain't," I say quietly.

"Yes we are!"

"You rob this bank and I'll trot right on over to the marshal and tell him just exactly who done it."

"Would he do that, Joshua?" She's sure some pissed.

"Yup."

Kim throws one bag back into the safe so it hits with a thud, then throws another.

"Ain't you gonna help?" she snaps.

"Why? I ain't the one took them out."

At that, Joshua walks silently out the door, which is just as well, leaving me alone with Kim and the money bags strewn over the floor. Kim grabs them all at once, heaves them into the safe, slams the door and spins the knob.

"There." She stands, slaps her hands together. "You satisfied?"

"Yeah. Thanks."

She comes at me, fists flying, lands one to the belly.

"You're the biggest bastard I ever knew, Pete Costello! My first God damn bank job, and you gotta go and screw it all up. This place is cake and you know it! We coulda made off with millions, more even, and all you can do is stand there and—Christ, I hate you!"

I've grabbed my stomach and half doubled over, though as much from laughing, or trying not to, as from Kim's left. She slugs me in the jaw next and I damn near fall over completely. I manage to grab her right wrist halfway through the third swing and duck in time to avoid a left hook that could knock my eye clear to the back of my head.

"Cut it out!" I holler, holding both her wrists now and not laughing so much. Not laughing at all.

She squirms, but I hold her and hope she don't start kicking. She don't, and after awhile I let go.

"It was a steal," she says. "So God damn easy. Why'd you have to blow it?"

"Because. Because it's what you said: too easy."

"What?"

"Too easy. It ain't worth it, don't you understand?"

"No I don't. I think you're selfish and dangerous and right now I don't care if I never see you again."

She takes off for the door but I grab her arm.

"You got a hell of a mean left," I say. "Did you know that?"

She glares and tries to yank away.

"Plus that right to the jaw."

"Let me go."

I hold on. She slaps me. I still hold on.

"Kim," I say, as gently as I can, "I'm sorry. I wish to hell it could've come off, but it's just too easy, and besides ain't nothing in it but hurting afterward, for us and for the folks who put that money here. God knows I've cussed them longhorns to hell and back, but I'd rather head off a stompede any day than do something like this. No chase, no shooting, no posse. It's low and dirty, so what's the good of it? You broke into the bank and cleaned out the safe; what difference does it make if you ride off with the money or not? It'll only weigh down your horse."

She stops struggling and stands real still, staring at me in that funny way. Then she reaches out and rubs my belly.

"Did it really hurt?"

"I said it did."

"Good." She leans closer to me. "Will you please kiss me? We might as well do something while we're here."

I do, hard and deep. Her body is warm and ready against mine, and we lie on the floor with the wood rough underneath, and I unbutton her shirt and she unbuttons mine, and then our trousers until about all that's left are our bandanas. And then damn if she don't let me take her, right there on the floor of the bank.

SEVEN

That's how we got arrested. See, after all that excitement the whiskey wore off, so we finished the bottle I brung into the bank and then fell asleep. Good thing we put most of our clothes back on first, because the owner of the bank got enough of a jolt when he tripped over us in front of his safe.

So now we're behind bars and my head hurts near as bad as yesterday, and I'd kill for one of Rosalie's biscuits and even for that fresh smooth coffee. Mostly I'd kill to get out of here, because these bars and this six-by-six cell make me nervous as a coyote stuck on a bob-wire fence.

One of the deputies saunters our way and you can tell he ain't too thrilled about drawing morning duty. Seems to be letting people out, though. He gets to Kim and me and looks us over and kind of guffaws.

"Ain't you Pete Jackson?"

"Christ," I say. "You been up the trail too? How come everyone knows who I am?"

He shrugs. "Word gets around. Lotta cow folk in town. Who's she?"

"Alice," I say.

Kim scowls.

"Just Alice?" asks the deputy.

"Just Alice," I tell him.

Kim scowls again.

"What the hell was y'all doing in that bank?"

"Robbing it," says Kim. "What the hell do you think?"

He unlocks the door and we walk out of there, and inside me that snake slinks off to the brush and my palms are cold and wet as hell but I don't let on. Kim and I walk to the hotel cantina and there's Rosalie waiting for us with a big grin on her skinny, blotchy face.

"Heard y'all landed in jail," she says.

"Word gets around," Kim replies.

"Righto," I say and we set to downing coffee and biscuits dunked in honey, and after that we go upstairs to find Joshua setting on the porch with his feet up, watching the street and puffing on a shuck.

"Heard you got arrested," he says, without turning around.

EIGHT

Roundup and horse-breeding season starts in early March at Rancho Renova, so we arrive in San Fernando by late February, having took the long way around and brung Kim with us. I figure she can go up the trail as good as any vaquero.

I also bring that red stallion, which is risky seeing how he might get pretty snaky back on his home range. He gets excited when we hit the east slopes and it's about all I can do to hold him. He takes to swinging that fine Arab head around and trying to take a chunk out of my leg, but I don't allow none of that.

Last day of the trip we only got a few hours riding, so we pick up some whiskey in the next village north and by the time we hit San Fernando we feel just fine. I reach over and swipe Kim's hat off and mess up her hair, which is shoulder length now, and she laughs and shoves me so I nearly fall off Red, who takes the opportunity to try and bite me again.

"Cut it the hell out, Red," I say, and tilt my head back for a long pull on the bottle.

Joshua sits straight and quiet on his black horse, nearly looking grim. Then again maybe it ain't grim, because I swear he's trying not to smile. Truly, I believe he's stifling a grin.

"Hey, Alice, what's got Chiso laughing?" I say.

Kim looks around me at Joshua. "What's so funny, Joshua?"

He makes no reply, goes on grim-like but really laughing, or so it seems, and looking straight ahead.

"What the hell," says Kim, and starts singing some Godawful trail tune loud enough to raise the dust and bring the monks out of their cells. I join her, but sounds like we got two songs going. We take to laughing so hard I about fall off Red. After a minute I look ahead, and now I see what has Joshua so amused.

Chickens skitter out of the way and of course we've picked up half the local dogs. Little kids watch with big liquid eyes in dark faces, squatting against buildings and maybe scratching the dust with a stick. A couple of old señoras stop cackling at each other and pull their rust-color rebozos tighter as we pass; one gives us a toothless grin and we nod to her.

But what's got Joshua amused is Mercedes. She stands in front of the cantina eyeing us and shaking her head. She has her hands on her hips and her rebozo draped across her shoulders, not wrapped around her, and her dress open pretty low, but she ain't looking at me. She's looking at Kim. I recollect giving some thought to this meeting over the weeks past, but maybe not enough. So I swing off Red, holding the saddle horn a second to keep my balance. I bow good and low, sweep off my hat. When I get standing straight again Mercedes finally looks at me instead of Kim.

"*Buenos días, Bella,*" I say.

"Eleven in the morning and already you are drunk."

Red nips my shoulder. I shove him away and reach for Mercedes. We press together from mouths to toes and kiss. She makes it good, which comes as no surprise.

"I have missed you," she whispers. "You did not come to visit this winter."

"I know, I know. We have been traveling. We are tired."

I look around at Kim and Joshua, who sit their mounts. Kim looks real sober for someone who could hardly stay in the saddle a few blocks ago. Looks kind of pissed, too. Joshua still looks grim and amused, one on top of the other, like there's a little flame clear at the back of his blackrock cave eyes. Kim urges her gray forward and stops right in front of Mercedes but don't dismount, just stares down at us. Mercedes looks pretty sober, too, downright icy, truth is.

"Mercedes," I say, "this here's Kim. Kim—"

"Obliged," Kim says in the same tone she'd tell anyone else to go to hell.

Mercedes laughs, but ain't no mirth in it. "*Buenos días,* Bellaca. *Buenos días,* phantom cow thief of Rancho Renova. So pleased to meet you." She faces me. "You have brought her in for the sake of justice, Costello? How kind of you. I know how much you hate rustlers."

"You—" Kim starts.

"Hold it," I say, and the whiskey drains partway out of my head. "I got some business with Mercedes here, so Kim, you just go have a drink at the cantina. It's on the house."

Kim sucks a deep breath and glares at me. Before she or Mercedes can say another word, I grab Mercedes by the elbow and hustle her to the back room. I figure Joshua will take care of Red and God knows Kim will take care of the cantina. Maybe there will even be something left by night.

In the sunbleached back room Mercedes wheels on me.

"Exactly what do you think you are doing, bringing that—" she flings an arm toward the cantina—"that child here? It is bad enough that she is a common thief, but when I see there is more . . . more between the two of you. . . . Oh, you are such a vile son of the greatest whore of them all!"

I sit tiredly on the scrubwood chair. "Christ, Mercedes, what is wrong with you? What does it matter if I have some girl riding with me? I am spending the night here, right?"

She stares hard at me. Her hair hangs like a black cape all around her shoulders and back and breasts, and the sunlight bouncing around the room pulls red from underneath the black. Her lips are pressed together and her eyes are narrowed, fiery in her dark face.

"Are you?" she says, hostile.

I sigh. "*Seguro.* I am."

A smile makes its slow way up her face. She don't part her lips on account of them two bad teeth, but it's still a smile.

"Only the night, Costello?"

I smile too. Mercedes lets her rebozo fall, swings her heavy, curly hair to behind her shoulders and undoes the next button on her dress, though God knows she had it better than half open already. She sits on my lap and I finish with the buttons, inch my fingers into her dress, stroke her breasts. She moves her shoulders and I slide the top of the dress off them and those big brown nipples are hard in the middle of all that melon roundness.

I kiss her on the lips, then the neck. Glass shatters against the other side of the wall. Kim. I pull back a little, but Mercedes laughs quietly and draws me close, and my hands work the buttons on the lower half of her dress while my mouth sucks one tight brown nipple.

Late afternoon Joshua and I stand in the middle of the cantina with Kim sprawled on the floor at our feet.

"Looks like she had one too many," I say. "Better get her out of here before the vaqueros arrive."

"Mercedes' room?"

"Mercedes is in there."

"Store room?"

"I think that's where she keeps the knives."

"She's got a gun, Pete."

I half smile. "Knife can do more damage, Chiso."

He still has that grim look with the amusement behind it. Together we carry Kim to the store room to sleep it off. God knows how she got falling-down drunk when the liquor's all over the walls. Smells up the whole room, too. Them vaqueros will be some pissed when there ain't enough to drink tonight.

"When I told her it was on the house this ain't exactly what I meant."

"Oh."

"Where were you, anyway? I thought you might try to calm her down."

He rights an overturned chair and sits in it. "Here. In this chair."

"Watching?"

"Well, I had a drink too."

"Glad you enjoyed yourself, Joshua." He weren't here and I know it. No way was he here.

I sit opposite him, pick a shot glass off the floor and pour Jack Daniel's from a broken-necked bottle. Hope there ain't no glass in it.

"Hell," I say. "Just hell."

I wake up with a start the next morning and try to figure what woke me. Dawn has long since passed and all seems quiet. Sun streams in on me, dust dances in the rays. I sit up and stretch. I'm alone in the room.

Then I hear Mercedes shout in the cantina: "You are nothing but a childish, petty little thief!"

And Kim: "A thief! Ha! Well, I would much rather steal cows than men. And you a *puta,* the lowest of women. Tell me, does he pay you in gold? Or just cheap tokens stamped with your name? How is it for whores in Mexico? I would not know."

I fall back on the rawhide and close my eyes. God damn them.

"He does not pay me." Mercedes' voice smolders now, hot

enough to melt a running iron. "If you think about it he pays you instead. I am his mistress, you are his whore."

Slap.

I get up, yank on my trousers, buckle on my gunbelt, and head for some fresh air. I walk behind the cantina and a row of jacales, snatch up empty tin cans along the way. I hear children, some laughing, others whining, and mothers snapping at them in Spanish. I hear hens cluck and goats bleat and two male dogs growl as they battle over a bitch. I chuckle at that. I hear the wind breathe through prairie grass and rustle through brush. But I don't hear Mercedes and Kim, not any more.

I set six cans on top of a boulder. I step back thirty paces, pull my Colt from its holster, my left hand slams the hammer six times. One can, not six, springs from the boulder and wrenches at each strike. The shots boom as one, and as the roar rolls off toward the mountains and the smoke makes my eyes smart, the can clanks to the gravel and San Fernando turns silent.

Then a cat yowls and a woman shrills at her daughter: *"Niña! Niña, ven aquí!"*

The other noises resume. I put a sixth can next to the remaining five and back up thirty paces. I reload, each bullet going in with a click, and reholster the gun. Mercedes should've expected this. I draw. Kim should've known too. I fire. Mercedes has always been a good friend. I fire again. And a better lover. And again. But Kim is different. Again. Maybe she even loves me. A fifth time my gun booms. All the cans still sit on the boulder, like they're staring at me but making no plea for mercy, like they want to get shot, damn it.

"The hell with them both," I say, and thumb the hammer. The sixth can jerks backward, struck, and topples.

So I walk slowly to the cantina, the Colt heavy and warm in my hand. In the back room I put on boots, shirt, vest, Stetson. I strap spurs to the boots and knot a red bandana loose around my neck.

Ain't a sound from the cantina and I wonder where those women are. Well, the hell with them, that's all. Let them fight. Let them claw like panthers and tear each other's hair until both are ugly and spent. Let them both follow me if they want, but don't let them expect me to wait. I'm heading for Don Vicente's and I'm staying there until the end of time, maybe longer. Hell with all women, all fences, all mother-fucking snakes.

I ride out on Red.

NINE

Don Vicente Renova owns most of northeast Coahila because he has lots of money and even more horses and cows, but also because no one else wants it. Ever since they made Diaz president and his men joined Don Vicente's to take out Juan Cortina and the other big bandidos, Don Vicente Renova's been king up here. He controls it all, even San Fernando's monastery: the head priest is his brother.

The don ain't ever married or fathered any children, far as I know, but he gets on fine with women as friends. Likes Mercedes right well, always gives her presents: blue porcelain wash set, fine liquor, poppy-color dress with black lace brought from Spain. Never sleeps with her, though his brother the priest does.

So the monastery rules the female half of San Fernando and Mercedes rules the male half, which means Don Vicente rules it all.

I gallop Red past the high stone arch that marks the west entrance to Rancho Renova's main hacienda. Dust puffs from Red's hooves as we pass, blurring the arch. The hacienda is a half mile farther along a well-trampled road lined with big mesquite trees and chunks of sandstone. The house itself is low 'dobe, like a fort, with a tiled roof and a courtyard in the middle. Truth is it ain't much to look at from outside. Used to be a bandit stronghold not too far back.

I pull Red in harshly, so he tosses his head and rears up a bit. He's about as itchy as I am. One of the ranch's *muchachos* runs to us, little boy in a white tunic and baggy trousers, barefoot though it's still some cool out.

"Hola, Señor Jackson," he says.

I get down and hand Red over to him. If anyone can handle that horse it's a ten-year-old Mexican born in the saddle.

The hacienda sits on a low rise. From this west side you can see San Fernando five miles off, with the monastery perched on the hill and the jacales squatting below, then many miles farther to the Sierra. Stock grazes here and there: single-color horse manadas northwest, big herd of cattle more south. Don Vicente runs upwards of 60,000 head of cattle, by book count: Texas longhorns mixed with Mexican stock and a bunch of wild black Spanish cattle that keep to themselves except when forced to breed with the others. Don Vicente lets the stock run pretty wild, only castrates the longhorn and Mexican bull calves every other year and never the black bulls, which would as soon gore a vaquero as mount a cow.

One of the house servants, who are all boys or men, leads me through an archway to the courtyard and says Don Vicente will be right along. I ask if he's seen Joshua and he says no, so I wait on the porch that surrounds the courtyard, which is a garden of shrubs and trees and flowers from the coast and on south, and smells moist and sweet. In the middle of the garden are a couple of big old parrots in bright blue and yellow and about every other color, and I know from earlier visits they speak Spanish as polite as a duke.

I hear a movement behind me and Don Vicente says, "Joshua is in the southern pasture assembling a remuda."

I turn to him.

"How are you, Pete?" We shake hands. He has the best manicured hands I ever seen, better than any woman's, smooth and brown and dry, but his grip is steel. Ain't real tall nor big, more trim, more like that red stallion I ride: small and quick and dangerous if you ain't careful. But I've never had to be careful around him.

He offers me a long cigar sent from some place special, lights mine and lights one himself, holds his in his wide mouth between thin lips and white teeth. He has one of them narrow black mustaches and eyebrows as fine, and his hair is short and thick, oiled back, tending to gray now that he's well into his fifties. You'd never think he was that old though: no wrinkles.

"I'm all right," I tell him. We usually speak English. He speaks a couple of other languages too.

"You seem a bit *agitado.*"

"I guess. Whose remuda?"

His black-eyed gaze darts over the courtyard. "Ryan Buckley's."

I chuckle at that. Buckley ain't never paid for a remuda in his life. Runs nothing but wet stock and trades off rustled herds with border bandits. The bandits steal from Rancho Renova and turn the stock over to Buckley's rustlers, then sell the Texas stock in Mexico. Neat system, but horse thieves don't live too long. Buckley's an old bank-robbing pard of Joshua's and so is his lackey, Sheriff. Ryan is okay but Sheriff is an asshole.

"How come Ryan's paying?" I ask.

Don Vicente raises his eyebrows and puffs on his cigar. "Your guess is as good as mine. Maybe better."

"Yeah." Cigar tastes right good. We walk slowly along the wood porch. After several paces Don Vicente sits on a bench facing the garden and crosses his legs. He has on black pants, neatly creased, and a brocade jacket. Told me once he gets all his clothes from Spain.

I lean on the railing that separates the porch from the garden, smoking. In the middle of the garden is a fountain with a marble statue of the Virgin above it, a small statue, and the way she looks down you might think someone hollered at her. Her features are long and soft and curved just so, and she has that shawl on her head like on all statues of her: I was raised Catholic and seen plenty.

"Is something wrong, Pete? I'll send a boy after Joshua if it is an emergency."

"No, I'll go myself. What do you call that flower out there? The red one with the snout coming out the middle." I point the cigar at it.

"That is a hibiscus."

Looks violent, or angry anyway, especially next to the Virgin. I nod slowly and draw on the cigar.

Another little while passes, then Don Vicente says, "How is Mercedes this morning? She was anxious for your return."

"Mercedes has her hooks in."

He chuckles. "And Bellaca?"

"Her too." I turn to face him. "But that ain't unusual, is it?"

"I think it is, this time. You aren't like this at other times. You have never cared before."

Damn if I care now. "I better go after Joshua."

He stands. "Maybe you'd like a drink first? Something with mint?"

"No. Thank you." I start toward the archway.

"Pete," says Don Vicente, "I do not think you and Joshua should take that remuda to Texas. I don't trust this Ryan Buckley or his friend Sheriff."

"I have to go," I say. "I'll be back in time to take a cow herd north if you want, but I have to go to Texas."

I leave the hacienda and ride to where Joshua trains the horses and set to helping him, and by supper we're pretty sore from the bucking. We ain't hardly said a word all afternoon, not even about the horses, but as the sun fades over the mountains I tell Joshua how Don Vicente don't want us to go.

"It's only Ryan and Sheriff," he says, and I could swear he's some irritated I even brung it up. So I let it lay, we get supper at the main hacienda, and next day we're back out with the horses.

Takes around a week to shape all 130 of them, and even then they're only half-broke. Meanwhile, Renova's vaqueros have started the roundup and castrating the bull calves, this being the year for it. They'll put together four trail herds totaling maybe 11,000 beeves. Don Vicente's already made his yearly trip north and has buyers lined up for all the herds; prices can't touch last year's, which is why he's only sending 11,000. Last year he sent three times that. I'll take one of the herds and Texas drovers will take over the other three at the border. I'm trailing clear to the Dakotas again, like last year, and figure to take pretty much the same corrida, seeing as how there ain't much work around the ranch midsummer and Renova vaqueros are the best anywhere. I guess Kim can still go if she wants. For all I know she might've left San Fernando by now. In a way I hope she stayed, but only in a way.

Joshua and I wind up the week soaking in hot tubs at the hacienda. Don Vicente arranges a noontime feast and we plan to rest a couple days before setting out. Driving that remuda should be okay: we only have to go as far as Carrizo Springs, this side of it at that. Brasada's some thick between the Rio Grande and there, but we're used to it.

So we wash and sit down to the feast. Don Vicente has on his Sunday best, or whatever's proper at noon, and his help have washed our clothes so that together I figure we three could go on stage. Table's laid with all kinds of vegetables and meats and a paella with freshwater mussels dotting the saffron yellow rice. I ain't seen such a meal since I got back from Dakota last September. Pretty as hell, and of course the best wine from the cellar flowing free as that Virgin statue's fountain.

By midafternoon we're so full we nearly roll around the floor, and half-crocked to boot, having switched to cognac and finally Irish whiskey. Nothing like Irish. We set to playing five-card draw with cattle for stakes, and Joshua wins a decent-sized herd. There'd be no stock at Tridente if not for Don Vicente's liquor cabinet and Joshua's skill with the cards.

Late at night the boy servants bring supper and more to drink. We pick at the food, still full from dinner. Don Vicente's sobered up a bit, not much.

"I would like to send Guillermo and Jose with this remuda," he says, and I realize he's more sober than he lets on. "Buckley has no interest in them and they are good with their guns. Any bandidos will be sorry to fool with them."

"Any bandidos will be sorrier to fool with us," I say. "And besides, those rustlers ain't near as thick as they used to be. Hell with them, I ain't worried about it."

"Actually, neither am I. It's your friends Buckley and Sheriff that worry me. Won't you consider staying here?"

"No," says Joshua, and that's the end of that.

Next morning I ride into San Fernando to see if Kim's still around. Maybe I don't care as much as I should, but I guess she could come along if she wants to. If she's still here and Mercedes ain't killed her, that is.

When I get to the cantina Mercedes is in there sweeping. She smiles at me kind of warm, her lips closed of course. I kiss her and she returns it, plus runs her hand over my back and down around the front, but that's all. Seems right friendly, so I figure Kim's took off.

"Kim has left?"

"She is still asleep. What would you like?"

I'll be damned.

"Coffee?"

"Yeah. Sure." I say it in English. Huh. "Where is she?"

"In the back room, sleeping."

"Oh."

She brings two steaming cafecitos and sets a bottle of Bushmill's Irish next to mine. I look at the bottle and at her, open the bottle and add to the cafecito until it almost overflows the cup. Mercedes sits across from me looking contented and I can't figure about Kim.

"How is Don Vicente?" Mercedes asks, smiling over her cup.

"Fine. No, he is worried."

"He is a mother hen."

"Sometimes."

"What worries him, Costello? Ryan Buckley's remuda? Or you?"

"Not the Remuda. You knew about that already?"

She says the vaqueros mentioned it last night.

"He does not want us to take it to Texas. He wants Guillermo and Jose to go. He does not want us to go back to Texas so soon."

"I do not think it wise, either. But you never listen, so all we can do is worry. At least it is something."

"I wish you would not worry."

"*Por qué?* It is good to have someone worry about you."

"Not if you worry about the person worrying."

She puts her hand on mine. I still can't figure her out. Nothing unusual shows in her eyes, no scheming, though she can cover right well.

"Do you worry, Costello? I did not think you worried so much."

"Everybody worries. Sometimes. But I still wish you would not."

"Kim worries."

"Kim?" I'm surprised to hear her use Kim's real name.

"*Sí, claro.* She—"

"She shouldn't." English.

Mercedes says nothing more but keeps her hand on mine, so I hold it loosely and drink the coffee and Irish. Nothing goes down like Irish.

The curtain to the back room parts and Kim comes in. Her eyes are puffy from sleep and her freckles stand out more than usual. She's dressed like the first and last times I seen her, except without gunbelt and leggins.

"Hi, Pete," she says like we seen each other ten minutes ago.

"Morning."

She pours herself a cafecito, joins us at the table and tops off the cup with some Irish. No one says anything and I start to feel some uncomfortable with the easy way these women are acting.

"Joshua and I got that Buckley remuda all ready to go," I say at last. "Figure to ride out tomorrow."

"Yes," says Kim. "I figured that too."

We speak English, but Mercedes don't seem to mind. Probably understands more'n she lets on.

"Want to come?" I ask Kim.

"You need a third hand?"

She knows damn well two can handle those horses. "No, just if you want."

"Vaqueros talk like it could get rough."

"Rough, hell."

Kim and Mercedes glance at each other. I get up.

"I'll be back inside two weeks, then it's north. You want to join my corrida, Kim, I'll make sure the vaqueros don't think you're a boy."

"Bastard," says Mercedes, in English, and ain't no smile on her now. Nor on Kim.

"Right," I say, and then I leave.

TEN

The Brasada on the Texas side is a whole lot worse than in Mexico, and horses can be harder to drive than steers. Lots of places the black chaparral reaches near twenty feet high, closes over your head like a net of thorns. Sun filters through, but it's harsh as light glinting off a knife. Thorns stab at your horse's feet, sometimes seems like someone pokes them out as you ride past. Spooky place, closes around you, a wall in front, a narrow tunnel behind that seals tight after you pass.

You listen to every sound in the brush, every crackle, every swish, every pop. You learn to tell the passing of your own horses from someone else's, some bandido who might take an interest in your stock. You learn to tell the rattles especially: you watch prickly pear, low brush, moist places, and steer clear. I can hear a rattle over a whole herd crashing through, learned to as a boy and never been bit.

You learn to know where other snakes hide, too, the snakes they call ladinos, wild longhorns who stand so still you might never see them, who only come out at night for water, who will stompede in terror at feeling full sunlight or the rope of a man. Sometimes they attack, their horns two more thorns in a forest of them, daggers that can hook you through and fling you clear above the brush. That's when you burst out and see the sky and you know how them snaky beasts feel when they get hit with full sun. Or the rope of a man.

We trail that half-wild remuda through this Brasada, alternating brush with wide pastures, about thirty miles into Texas, to the near side of Carrizo Springs. We move slow to spare the stock, especially in the thickets, and camp the first night in the open with a rope corral for the horses and fried steak and cornbread for supper. The aroma of sweetbriar blows from the thicket at our backs. Stars come out, no moon, and the temperature dips low before dawn, when we get up and move on into the paling world.

We trail out of a white brush draw onto the rolling prairie that Ryan Buckley has claimed for his ranch. It's a fair size and surrounded by thickets. Buckley has dodgers on him, but he don't use an alias and no one down here tangles with him. Or Sheriff.

From the edge of the thicket we can see the 'dobe jacal Ryan and Sheila call their own. I figure they stole it from some Mexican peon, or maybe a bandit, then built the barn. Barn is newer, of oak brought from farther east. Woodpile runs along one side, and there's brush and cactus growing here and there. Ain't no bunkhouse, because Ryan hires different corridas for roundup and rustling and suchlike, never keeps a regular corrida, only that bastard Sheriff.

"Getting fancy," I comment on the series of fenced pastures and corrals that surround the house and barn. Corrals are built of sturdy wood posts and planks; pastures are fenced with bobwire. Longhorn stock grazes in groups in the pastures, must be near 4,000 head spread out. All colors, the way longhorns are, and likely all brands, too.

"When were we here last?" I ask.

"Two years."

Joshua looks grim like when we got to San Fernando, but no amusement under it this time.

The door to the 'dobe house opens and three people come out to watch us. Rancho Renova raises the best horseflesh between the Big Bend and the Gulf of Mexico, so I'd bet this remuda makes a pretty sight trotting over the low rolling terrain between us and the house. We dip between hills and the house disappears except for the chimney smoke, then up again and you can see it closer, plus the three people in front: the wiry man is Ryan, the plump woman is Sheila, and the tall broad-shouldered man is Sheriff.

Ryan and Sheila ain't married, never have been, though Carrizo knows them as the Buckleys. Her name is Sheila McCrory, and I've heard tell she and Ryan killed her husband, who was also supposedly a rustler. But then I'm supposed to have killed my own brother. That's the way of it here: stories, lots of lies, lots of folks no one knows except for the stories, and to hell with most of the stories. Most of the people too. But not all, because stories do lie.

Anyway Ryan's probably in his forties, jumps around like a kangaroo rat, never still. Always working his mouth or tugging his chin or swiping his gun-barrel gray hair back along his head. Usually has the look and smell of a man who's worked up a sweat asking a compadre for money, but truth is he's tough through and through, not like Sheriff, who's a coward, or like Sheila, who seems always scheming to protect her own interests. She'd as soon try to kill Ryan, I expect, if she saw some gain in it, but she has to know she'd never live through trying. No one tangles with Ryan.

Sheila looks to me like a merry woman, like you'd see serving up a big apple pie or plate of cookies, but a merry woman in a bad mood, still with the plump red cheeks, but *agitado* in the eyes. She does make good apple pie, as I recollect, but the bad mood never ends: she's pretty much a bitch.

As for Sheriff, if not for him Andy'd still have the lower half of his right arm.

Ryan points to a streamfed pasture near the barn and we turn the remuda into it. They fidget a minute, then set to sucking the water and gnawing the grass like they was born here. By the stream yellow wildflowers bloom, and for reasons I'd rather not wonder about they set me to thinking of Kim.

Then Sheriff walks over and says, "How y'all doing?" and Kim's the last person on my mind.

"Howdy, Sheriff."

Joshua nods: he has no more love for Sheriff than I do.

We dismount and lead our horses toward the barn. Ryan and Sheila come over and we shake hands.

"Morrals are in the barn," says Ryan, glancing around and working his mouth. "Any trouble?"

"Nope."

"No bandidos?" says Sheriff. He always has to push.

"Nope," I say again.

Sheila presses her lips together like she's pissed, but that's just her. She'll think of something to say sooner or later, but only because she'll figure she ought to make conversation and not because she enjoys it. I ain't sure what Sheila enjoys.

Inside the barn smells like stale hay and horse piss. No horses in here now, must be in a corral out back. Barn ain't too big, four stalls and a loft, plus pegs on one wall for tack. Sun comes through cracks in the wood. We fill morrals with corn, water the horses, and hang the morrals under their muzzles. I left Red at Renova, of course. All he needs is a devil's head thorn to cripple him or some bandit to steal him.

Inside the 'dobe house we set round a rough table on benches and pass a bottle of tequila. We catch up on whatever's happened the last two years, but it ain't a lot and comes off a heap more interesting with some made-up parts thrown in. You can pretty well get to the bottom of a story by tossing the best three-quarters, if you want.

Sheriff does most of the talking, though I don't recollect him being such a talker. Sheila rustles some chuck, so that soon the tallow smoke sends us men outside. After awhile Sheriff works around to what I figure he's wanted to ask all along.

"Hear y'all got some kid riding with you."

"Yeah?" I say. "How old? I mean, you talking about a real little kid?"

Ryan darts a nervous glance at me: he don't want trouble. Guess I don't owe him none, either.

"Maybe a girl kid," says Sheriff. "Though folks ain't too sure."

"Folks, huh. Who y'all think she is, Sheriff? Who do folks say she is?"

Sheriff looks kind of hard at me. "Don't get smart with me, Pete. I ain't meaning no harm."

I laugh and reach for the tequila. "Me neither. I just want to know what stories are floating around."

He gets a slow smile on his face. Looking at him now I figure the ladies might think he's some handsome, with them blue eyes and dark hair and a square jaw. I think he's an ass.

"Some folks figure she's Bellaca. That about right?"

I drain the tequila. "Truth is, Sheriff, I got no one but Joshua riding with me, and no need for any cow thief, girl or otherwise."

Sheriff rises a little like he's fixing to hit me but Ryan clears his throat and that's that.

"I'll pick up the money for the remuda in Carrizo tomorrow," he says in his raspy voice. "You boys plan to lay over a couple of nights, don't you?"

"Yup," says Joshua, and we head back inside to eat.

Sheila serves beans and fried steak, fresh baked bread and more tequila to wash the lot down. For dessert she pours sizzling tallow over blackstrap, and the hardening tallow sticks to the roof of our mouths. No one talks much during the meal, except for pass me this or that, and after dessert we're busy sucking the tallow out of our mouths with our tongues.

"Pete here's had Bellaca riding with him," Sheriff tells Sheila.

"Hand me your plates," she says.

"Guess he left her at Renova, huh Pete?"

I can see Sheila ain't interested. I light a cigarro, Joshua lights a shuck, and Sheriff lights a cigarette. Ryan don't smoke, just works his mouth and looks around nervously.

"Nice supper, Sheila," I say. "Ladino?"

She half smiles. Beef with that strong gamy flavor has to be ladino. No ranch-bred longhorn tastes that good.

"So how come she stayed back, Pete?" says Sheriff. "Y'all have a little squabble?"

"Sheriff?" I say, real mild and polite.

"Yeah?"

"Would you please go fuck a cow?"

Well, he like to rise right off that bench and stomp across the table so he's looking down at me, with his hands on his hips. He decides to kick and I'm all ready to turn him ass up, which he is already if you think about it. I stay sitting.

"Y'all look kind of comical up there," I say with the cigarro in my teeth. "Find a mouse under the table or something?"

He swings a foot toward my jaw. I grab it and jerk it around and he tumbles off the table onto the floor. I'm up now and he scuffles to find his feet.

"Can't you boys take this outside?" says Sheila. "I just cleaned this place."

"Looks right nice too," I tell her, and extend a hand toward Sheriff. He accepts it and I haul him to his feet. He gets up slow, then suddenly his big left fist rams into my gut. My cigarro goes flying and I start to double over, but only to throw him off. I hook him a left to the jaw. His head snaps back, he spins around, pots and pans clatter as he slams into them.

"Jesus Christ," Ryan mutters. "Go outside."

I'm all for it, but here comes Sheriff. I step out of the way and he lands on the half-cleared table. Comes up wearing dinner, or what's left of it. I start laughing and he slugs me true in the jaw, and when my head clears Joshua and Ryan are gambling at the table and Sheila's washing dishes. I'm lying on the floor where I landed and my jaw hurts. Sheriff must've gone outside. I get up and sit at the table and Joshua deals me in without a word.

We finish up cards and another bottle of tequila. Sheriff never does come back, and my jaw's some swelled by the time Joshua and I head for the barn. I figure it's worth the laugh. We make down our beds on the stale-smelling hay.

"It ain't your beef," Joshua says in the dark.

"No. But Andy ain't here."

"I reckon."

The hay crackles as he rolls over, and soon he breathes slow. I lie awake a long time, until I get bored and go outside. Joshua's breathing don't change but I know he wakes up when I leave. He don't sleep real sound.

Outside the stars make a million holes in the sky but with no moon it's a damn dark night. I hear critters scurry and scratch and some bird calling. Remuda sleeps in that pasture to the west: I can smell them on the light breeze. All else is silent, as silent as any night can get. I feel kind of spooky, like how you feel when someone watches you or a sudden cool air blows across the back of your neck.

So I decide to take a stroll around the barn. The grass is dry and you can hear it fold underfoot. I tread real light and slow. After a minute I draw my six-shooter, though a lot of good it will do with no moon. Damn but it is dark.

I walk to the side of the barn with the woodpile along it. I hear a rustle, then a creak, a creak of leather, like maybe of a man's leggins. Then the wind shifts and slips around the corner of the barn and hits me full with the smell of a whole bunch of men.

They ain't seen me or heard me or they would've moved. I'm right by the woodpile. I take another step and crack a stick. One of them whispers something I don't catch and I hear them sneak around the corner toward me. They must've been behind the barn.

I drop back to where the woodpile ends and squat with my gun drawn and my back against the barn. They could be bandits or they could be after us. Or Ryan, he's wanted too. I have to warn Joshua and Ryan and Sheila. Hell with Sheriff: if they're after us I'd lay odds he's leading the attack. But I think they're bandits, followed us in here and want them horses.

I put my left hand down to steady myself. Something grabs my arm. Something sharp. Then something else, sharper. And more. I want to scream. I can feel them pump venom into my arm. No rattles, no warning: baby rattlesnakes. Christ, I want to scream. Those men are right in front of me. Fucking rattlers won't let go. I raise my arm and they won't let go. The venom pumps in and I open my mouth and put my head back, and I want to shoot every one of those men. But I have to kill the snakes or they will kill me. I have to take the chance. I bring the butt of my Colt down on them, thudding.

The men jump and gasp and in the dark I see bulky forms turn toward me. The snakes let go and I start thumbing the six-shooter. The booms shatter the night.

One of the men cries out and they start shooting at where my gun made bursts of flame, but I'm not there, I'm racing around toward the front of the barn, holding my arm and feeling the venom course toward my shoulder. At the corner I collide with Joshua. Those men start shooting in our direction, but other directions too, you can tell by the flames from their guns. Then they stop, they don't know where we are.

Inside the barn we throw saddles on our mounts, who dance and snort.

"The barn!" I hear one of the men holler.

"Fuck, they ain't bandits," I say. "They're after us."

We swing into our saddles, jam our feet into the stirrups and our heels into the horses' sides, and bolt from the barn at a dead run. Bullets follow. We snap off a couple of shots but we mostly have to ride like hell.

"How many?" Joshua shouts.

"I don't know. Six or more."

We streak across the prairie. I glance back toward the house. No lights. No God damned lights.

My arm is fire and every hoof that hits the ground burns it more. I feel sick as hell already and Joshua don't even know it. I can't tell him now.

We have to watch out for bobwire. I can't see a thing except the stars and where they end at the horizon and, behind us, at the house and barn. Barn looks like a big black box in the middle of the starry sky.

No more shots now. Reckon they run back to get their horses. That'll buy us a minute; they expected to take us in the barn.

"Bobwire!" calls Joshua, and suddenly he's a black shape against the sky as his horse clears the fence. Then I'm airborne, nearly thrown but gripping with my knees and leaning into the jump. I have my coyote dun, best all-around horse in my string except for Red. Thank God I ain't got Red.

Hooves thunder behind us now. Rifle shots crack out. My dun stumbles, regains his feet, runs on.

"You all right?" Joshua calls.

"Yeah. He tripped."

We head for the thicket but if we go in here they'll follow the noise. They're close enough. I hate the idea of riding through that brush at night. Both our horses are night horses, but still.

Joshua swings south at the edge of the thicket. I follow. We been riding near twenty minutes, and I'm about all in. Joshua still don't know it. I ain't even got a tourniquet on that arm. Christ, I feel so sick. My mouth tingles real strange-like and my arm is numb around those three bites. They're close together. The rest of my arm burns. Every time I move it I want to scream.

"You all right?" Joshua calls again, farther ahead.

"No," I murmur to myself. "God, no." He can't hear that, I know.

"Pete?"

I realize my horse has slowed. I look back and see the men have split up. They have torches now. One half rides north along the thicket and the other half south, toward us. They move damn fast. I spur my horse and catch up to Joshua.

"Get into the thicket," I say.

"What's wrong?"

"Nothing. Get in."

We turn in. We have to go slower now. Brush crashes around us. Thorny branches switch my face, my arms, my legs, slashing. I lean on my horse's neck, use it as a shield but them branches whip me bloody. We have to get far enough in that those men don't hear the brush.

Joshua's horse stumbles, mine near runs him over. He gets up. Joshua stays on him. We keep going. Another couple of minutes and my stomach turns over. Joshua don't hear me slow down, he keeps going. The crashing shoots inside my head and makes it hurt, like thorns stabbing the backs of my eyes. I squeeze my eyes shut and open them but it's black as hell in here. My stomach turns over again, I feel real dizzy. I grip the saddle horn but still sway. The horse runs under a mesquite branch but I don't see it, I feel it, it swipes me off and I land on my back on a bed of thorns.

I don't even move, just close my eyes and groan and feel like death. Then I hear Joshua get off his horse and squat by me, but I can't see him it's so black in here. He touches me, hits my arm by mistake, and I jump.

"What's wrong?"

"Snakes. Fucking snakes."

"Christ."

He lights a match and peers at my arm, then around at the cactus. Thorny shadows dance in the small circle of light. The match goes out and Joshua rustles in the brush. I hear a slicing sound and he lifts my arm and jabs what feels like a knife into it. I bite my lip and taste salt from the blood. May be too late for the Spanish dagger's poison to help. Joshua don't bother with a tourniquet, too late for that too.

"Tie me on the horse."

"Thicket will kill the horses. Dawn ain't far."

I close my eyes but hell if it makes any change from the dark. Joshua rustles around some more, sounds like he chops brush a few feet away. He comes back, helps me sit up, and we move to where he cleared a spot.

"What a fucking mess," I say. My voice comes back slurred and weak. Joshua don't say nothing. It's cold here in the early morning; we left our blankets at Ryan's.

"Ryan's in on this," I say, and it's getting hard to talk.

"Or else he's dead."

"Yeah. Shit."

It's damn cold out here. I start to shiver, but ain't no help for it. No help at all, and God knows I'd sell my soul for a bottle of Irish.

ELEVEN

My arm catches fire, wakes me. Still dark. I move.

"Hold still," says Joshua. He cuts the sleeves of my jacket and shirt. They are so tight it feels like someone tied wet rawhide around my arm and set it by the fire to dry. I hold still.

Sun ain't up yet but the sky is blue, not black, above the thorns. I must've passed out or fell asleep. I'm cold as hell.

Joshua helps me get up. My whole skin has swelled, feels like the top layer has been scraped off. I can't walk too good. Joshua helps me to my horse and into the saddle, then climbs up behind me. But it ain't my horse, it's his black.

"Where's the dun?" I ask. Hard to talk with my face swelled. Hard anyway.

"He's lame." Joshua sounds sorry as hell. "Devil's head."

For the first in a long time, all I want to do is cry.

"Least it weren't Red," I say, and feel Joshua nod. That dun is a damn good horse, I've rode him three years. Damn good horse.

Joshua's black can hardly walk. Thorns have made him stiff,

takes awhile to loosen up. Damn about that dun. And the saddle. We move slow, let the black pick his way through the brush. I feel mighty sorry for him with both of us on top.

"Any sign of those men?" I manage to ask.

"They'll be along come dawn."

We ride on. No more'n a half hour until dawn. Thicket has lightened, you can make out colors. All looks kind of yellow to me, but that's from the snakebites. I look at my arm: two-three times its normal size, dark and mottled in this grainy predawn glow. Looks like a nest of baby rattlers wriggle inside it, feels like they bite it all the time. I close my eyes and let my chin fall forward onto my chest.

"Hang on," says Joshua. "We'll get there."

He sounds far away, like the cracking brush, like the whistles of the birds and footfalls of the horse. Horse starts to trot. I can't handle the pain from that so good. I try to clench my right fist, but no go, the fingers are too swelled, even on that hand. Horse breaks into a lope and I know we're out of the thicket but I don't care.

Seems like we go in and out of thickets all day and I keep passing out and coming to, and always we move. We never stop and we never rest. The sun swings overhead and drops down west, in our eyes, hurts my eyes even when they're closed. Horse keeps going at that lope, I don't know how he does it. Joshua looks back and says no sign of the men. At least it's something.

We cross the Rio Grande late in the afternoon. River's low and muddy. I get sick in it and after that my belly stays knotted and my body tries to turn inside out until I'm so tired I can't even pass out. Well into the night Joshua says, "There's Renova."

I force my eyes open and see blurred yellow dots ahead.

"Renova . . ." I hear myself whisper.

"Hang on," says Joshua.

Soon he climbs down. I feel the horse start to quiver and I know he'll die.

"Sorry, boy," I murmur.

I start to fall but a bunch of hands catch me. Somewhere off I hear Don Vicente ask what's wrong, then I hear him close to me and feel a warm dry hand on my face.

"Carry him inside," he says in Spanish. "Quickly. One of you bring my brother."

They lift me and begin to walk. I half open my eyes but it's too dark to see and the stars blur into each other. I try to talk but nothing comes out and I can't remember what I wanted to say. Then bright lights hit me and it's warm and the men set me on a bed. Don Vicente leans over me.

"You will be all right," he says, but I ain't so sure, not the way I feel and not when I heard him send for his brother.

"Irish," I whisper. "No priest."

Don Vicente looks like he tries to smile. He sends one of the boys after the Irish and soon holds my head and tilts the bottle to my lips.

"Right from the bottle," he says. "Drink up."

I can't take it so good. Most drips down my chin, wets my shirt, feels cold against my chest. Joshua stands across the room, sideways to me, runs a hand through his long lank black hair. He don't look my way, I don't think he can, and I want to thank him for bringing me back but I don't dare.

I must be coming and going, because next I know my eyes are closed and I hear a man mumbling. I can't understand the words. What the hell, I wonder. Maybe I am confused. Then I understand.

"Get out of here, priest," I say. "Leave me alone."

The mumbling continues.

"Get out."

"You should not talk like that, Pete." Don Vicente. "You are very sick."

"No priest."

When I open my eyes a second or an hour later, Kim stands over me. I feel my eyes move in my head, move over her body. I have made love to that body, to those small high breasts and narrow hips and the warm wet place between those short strong legs. I want to make love to you now, Alice Bellaca Kimberly. I want to feel what I felt making love to you, and not this pain. I look at her mouth, the small mouth I once thought was nothing special, but it could take away the pain, maybe, or help cover it. I feel my own lips part. Kim leans over and kisses me: carefully, gently, like she loves me, and for a minute I want her to love me. Her, or someone.

I sleep, and later I am a snake again, coiling in the corner of the barn and watching as Pa beats Mick. I watch like I would watch a man walk down the street: I feel nothing, no hatred. No venom. Mick cries out: "Peter Jack! Peter Jack!" He looks right at me as the fists raise red eggs on his skin, but I just watch. I do not care. I do not care, and that hurts, it scares me.

But I have to strike. I done it all the other times. Tired now, but no help for it: got to strike. But then I ain't a snake, I'm a boy with a gun and the gun burns in my hand. I raise the gun.

"Stop!"

He don't even look up.

"Peter Jack! Peter Jack!"

I raise the gun higher, look down the barrel. There's the snake, the barrel is a snake, with the tongue flicking out the end, toward the man killing the boy, toward my father murdering my brother.

"Stop!"

My brother falls to his hands and knees. Blood, thick and syrupy, drips from his mouth to the hay. Hay turns red. Pa hits him again. Pa is drunk. Pa is always drunk. Hits Mick again.

Mick lies down. Eyes close.

"Stop!"

Pa raises his fist.

I squeeze the trigger.

Pa's head explodes. Blood and bits of Pa's head spatter the hay, mix with Mick's blood. Pa falls on top of Mick.

"Peter Jack!"

But Mick is dead. He can't talk.

"Peter Jack!"

Behind me: Ma.

"I done it, Ma. He's dead. I done it for Mick."

But she has a gun. She raises the gun. Her eyes are small and round and black.

"He killed Mick, Ma. Pa killed Mick."

I step toward her. I try to explain. I spread my arms. Her eyes are small and round and black: I seen eyes like that before. I seen through eyes like that. They look down the gun barrel at me and her finger coils around the trigger.

I scream.

"Pete!"

I scream again.

"Pete!"

I open my eyes: Kim.

"She tried to kill me." I shake all over. Kim reaches under me and holds me. My heart beats against my chest, against Kim, like trying to get out.

"It's all right," she says. "It's only a dream."

The door opens and I see Don Vicente.

"He's all right," Kim tells him. "Only a dream." She lets me lie back. I still shake. Don Vicente closes the door with a click. Kim touches my face with a wet cloth. I feel sick and shaky and hot, like someone holds a torch to my skin.

"Tell me your dream," she says.

I look away. I cannot look at her eyes when they tell me she cares.

"Who tried to kill you?"

"My mother."

"Because you killed your father?"

"He killed my brother." I look at her. "Go away now. Leave me."

She presses her lips together, but her chin quivers anyway and her eyes shine. She shakes her head and stays there.

Healing takes a long time. The herds trail north before I get out of bed. Mercedes visits but never knows what to say. After awhile she stops coming. Joshua sets in the room smoking his shucks. After a few days I ask him for a cigarro and we smoke together. We hardly talk, and he looks grim and narrow-eyed. Some days he stands at the window, which looks east, and stares at Texas, and I can see snakes laying up in those blackrock cave eyes of his. I drink Irish and he stands watching Texas, waiting for me to get better so we can go back but all I get is drunk.

Kim tells me she works for Don Vicente. I ask the don and he says it's true. Joshua don't want to train horses, don't seem to care; Kim does it instead. We're short on cash, but Joshua stands at my window staring at Texas. I don't let on that I'd rather not go back. I just drink.

Kim visits at night, lies next to me in bed. After a week she touches me where she ain't touched since we left Juniper. I touch her, too, but healing takes a long time. Kim lies by me all night, every night. I lie awake and feel her curled at my side like a child, breathing like a child, and I think how she jumped on Red that first time. I see it in my head and it makes me sad, though I don't know why, so I reach for the bottle next to my bed. Irish sloshes in the bottle, noisy as a river in the night, sloshes down my throat.

Don Vicente says he's running out of Irish. Two weeks have passed and I can walk around the hacienda. I feel very weak, usually, like I got no bones. But I walk around. One day I look at the back pasture and there's Red, romping like a yearling. I whistle. He pricks his ears, nickers, bucks.

"Hey, Red," I say, and walk off to set in the courtyard listening to the parrots' polite chatter and the Virgin's fountain. Later I ask Kim if she's been riding Red.

"No," she says. "I ain't even tried."

"He's going back ladino."

"That's your problem."

That night she lies next to me, and when she touches me I feel the blood pulse and for a little while I am strong again. Makes me chuckle, though.

"What's funny?" says Kim.

"I ain't no gentleman. Gentleman takes his weight on both arms."

"You ain't anyway. Roll over."

I laugh again. Healing takes a long time, but the time is almost over now.

TWELVE

Joshua is some pissed when I refuse to go after Sheriff.

"We owe him," he says.

"We'll pay, but not now. Don't go alone, either." That's probably the only time I've ever told him what to do.

"We owe him," he says again.

"I want to go to Tridente. I can't get into no fight, not now."

He looks pissed but keeps quiet. He looks at the bed, just a glance, but I know he thinks of Kim. He thinks she makes me want to go to Tridente.

"It ain't Kim," I say. "I just don't want to fight. Not now. Maybe later. I'm tired of fighting."

He nods slowly. "You don't go later, I will."

"I'll go. But not now."

Before we leave I get on Red and ride into town to see Mercedes. Red has gone some wild but that's all right, I'm strong again and anyway I like him better wild. I walk into the cantina mid-afternoon but Mercedes ain't there.

"Mercedes?"

No answer.

I walk through to her room, my boots making a flat sound on the hard-packed dirt floor, my spurs clanking. The room is bare, swept, the rawhide and blankets in a neat roll against one wall.

"Mercedes?"

The back door is open. Ain't a door anyway, just a portal. She only strings rawhide across it in bad weather, and that ain't often. Sun's in front of the cantina now, so the building casts a shadow outside the back door. I stand in the room looking out: wildflowers in every color bloom from the prairie. I step outside and find Mercedes. She sits on that boulder gazing at the flowers.

"Hello, Pete Costello," she says, in English.

I touch her hair, black now with no red on account of the shadow.

"You are riding to Tridente, no?" Spanish, and still watching the prairie. "Today?"

"*Mañana.*"

"Yes. Always tomorrow. Always one more night. Except last time."

I sit on the boulder next to her and light a cigarro. "You stopped coming to see me."

She shrugs. "You were healing all right. There was no more danger."

"No."

I smoke.

Finally she says, "It is wise to go to Tridente. Better than Buckley's."

I nod.

"But you will go in the end."

"We have to."

"Yes, there is no other way. This world leaves you no other way."

"I know."

She laughs her terse "Ha," short and mirthless but not vicious. "I would like us to make love," she says, "one last time."

I smile. "I would like that too, Bella." But we don't, which I guess is just the way it goes. Instead I leave the next morning with Kim and Joshua and follow the short route through the Sierras. It is April and the desert on the west side blooms: bluebonnets, red flames atop spiny stalks, shower of gold, sunset pink cups on strawberry cactus. Birds gather wherever tinajas hold water, and at night coyotes howl in a chorus sweet to anyone who sleeps best under the stars.

We hardly have any money, just the little Kim made shaping remudas and what Don Vicente paid us for the trip to Buckley's. I figure he ought to kept that money, since Ryan never did pay us for the remuda. But he insisted. Then Joshua sold back the cattle he won at poker, so he has that. I come up shortest, especially after spending forty-five dollars on a new saddle. Least I have Red and the other two horses in my string. Red don't like the new saddle any more than I do: saddle takes longer to break in than a new horse and every time I mount up I think of that coyote dun.

I miss the trail too. Been up it near every year since leaving home, and that was thirteen years ago. Some years I started farther north, signed on at Red River Station or Dodge, but the last several I started in Mexico. Nothing like a trail drive: you love it and hate it, get bored and pissed and lonely and sick of folks and cattle all at once, but every year you come back for more.

But this year I ride west toward Tridente with Kim and Joshua, over the Sierras and into the flowering desert, across the muddy Rio with its slimy banks.

"Dry already," I comment at the river.

"Yup," says Joshua, and we cross.

"Andy'll be some surprised to see us," says Kim.

"Yup."

We head up the gentle sand and gravel rise toward Glenn Springs. The grass grows more sparse than usual. Even with the flowers the desert looks bare: flowers stand out stark against it. Must've had some rain but not much. Closer to Tridente the area looks just as bare. Feels bare too. No life.

"Stock must be farther up," I say. No grass down here.

We ride around that last little rise. Still no stock. I look at the three caves and the burned black mark above the middle one, then at the cabin. Cabin looks empty: no smoke but that ain't it, just looks empty. We ride closer and a smell comes on the breeze, faint, foul. Red tosses his head. I pat his neck and speak low to him. I feel Kim look at me. I look at Joshua. He stares ahead at the cabin, but his jaw has a knot.

We ride the horses into the corral, dismount. We leave the saddles on, the cinches tight. Silently we walk toward the cabin. The smell reaches us in small waves, faint on the breeze so you wonder if you imagine it.

We walk toward the cabin, the dry grass crackles under our feet, our boots break clumps of dry earth. Outside the cabin we stop. That smell ain't stronger, just all around now. Joshua puts out his hand and holds the rawhide door flap aside, and now the smell is plenty strong.

For us who still have it life becomes a string of sounds: axes echo off tree trunks, fir trees crash to the mountainside, metal blades saw back and forth, hammers crack.

Then silence, or only a rustle of the canvas-wrapped bundle against our clothes, the heaviness of our footfalls under the burden. But silence, mostly.

Then shovels slice into sandy, gravelly earth, toss it aside to land with small thuds, small enough so you can hear us breathe as we work. Sometimes a shovel strikes a rock: metal clanks against stone. And our breathing turns labored as we work it loose, heave it away.

Silence again. You try to shut off every sense with sound: sound hurts less. But in the silence the eyes open and you stare down that hole in the ground, and at the nailed shut box next to it, the nails black in sap-yellow wood. And you smell the wood and what's inside, though the canvas and the nails seal it tight.

Sound don't hurt unless you talk and no one talks. We stand still, for a moment letting the other senses come back to life, then slide ropes under the box, lower it, and sound returns: shovels slice the pile of earth, earth thumps loud and hollow on the box, then muffled, on itself.

The sounds run out and leave a little panic in their wake. We go inside and stoke the fire, open a can of tomatoes, and set some pinto beans in a pot with water and salt and chilipiquin peppers. Mix some cornmeal with water—ain't no tallow—and make hard cakes. Serve it but no one eats: taste hurts the worst.

Open a bottle of Jack's and pass it. Drink from tin cups, savor the sound of the Jack's sloshing in the cups. Drink up, lie back with the cup on your belly and the Jack's spreading inside. Lie back and work your ears to death making little sounds into thunder, but ain't no more'n the quiet pop of the fire as it dies, and somewhere far off a canyon wren's call.

THIRTEEN

We don't go back by way of Renova, no point in it. We rest three days at Tridente, then head out. All the stock is gone, sold already I'd bet. Not that there was so much but Andy made sure to breed the animals well, especially the horses but also the cattle. May rolls around while we ride and I think how in another month Rafaela will stop at Doan's and one of the drovers will tell her I ain't up the trail this year. I ought to gone up the trail and to hell with that remuda. To hell with having a price on your head and to hell with it all.

We camp in the thicket west of the Buckley place, ten miles out.

"Think that dun's around here?" I say. We build a small smokeless fire under a mesquite tree so no one will take notice.

Joshua draws on his shuck and says nothing.

"Maybe the saddle," says Kim.

"Yeah," I say. "Think Ryan's still alive?"

"Nope." Joshua and Ryan go way back, or that's what Andy always said.

Next day we sit our mounts at the edge of the thicket. I'm on a sorrel born in the Brasada, been riding him four years but he can't touch that dun or Red. I'd never take Red on a job like this: left him at Tridente, what there is of it, turned loose in the back pasture below them three holes. Ain't nobody going to tangle with him.

We can see the Buckley place from here, far off. Hard to tell how much activity there is, though you can see plenty of stock close to the buildings. Probably Renova stock, the sons of bitches. And that much stock means plenty of men around, bandits, likely, rustling bandits.

My sorrel brush horse shifts under me. Damn new saddle creaks. We trot our mounts out of the thicket and toward the ranch buildings. We have to get closer to see who's where and how many, but not too close or they'll see us. We dismount and walk on foot when the hills get high enough to show us against the sky. We leave the horses ground-reined in the last draw and lie on our bellies on a rise for a good view.

"Christ," I say.

"Must be twenty down there."

"Yup."

"Shaping up a trail herd."

"Late for that."

"Late, hell. Where'd they get the buyers? No one else can get buyers now, even early."

"We go around to the other side," says Joshua. "Wait until night to move in."

"Just like they done."

He squints at the sky. Big blue dome, no clouds.

"Full moon tonight," says Kim.

"Stompede the cattle."

Joshua nods, points to three places.

"Guards. They're expecting us."

"They might be soft now. They don't know about the snakes."

"No."

But they don't look soft.

"No vaqueros," I say. "All gringos."

"Yup."

"Recognize any, Joshua?"

"Yup."

"They'll bed the herd over there." I point to a high pasture a couple of miles from the house. You can tell by the green tint that they haven't bedded there before. "We come in upwind on an unbroke herd, shouldn't be too hard."

Joshua points to a remuda a short distance from the cattle.

"Not Renova stock," I say, "but they'll do."

"If we have time," says Kim.

"Won't nobody chase us this time. Won't be nobody left."

"Recognize all of them, Joshua?"

His jaw twitches. "Some."

"I don't want killing where it ain't needed."

"Then aim for the rest."

"Joshua."

He looks hard at me. Hard and grim, and snakes in those blackrock cave eyes. You can nearly hear them hiss.

"We ain't killing unless we have to. Sheriff we have to, but he'll know it first."

"You're getting soft," he says, quiet as can be.

I look at him a long time, but ain't no help for it.

Next day we circle to east of the ranch. I ride ahead to scout the herd. They're spread over six acres or so, grazing easy. Boys'll throw them together at night, probably; they done it last night. Being near the herd sets me to wishing for the trail again. Be nearly to Doan's by now. Doan's, but Rafaela too, and I kind of wish that if I had gone up I'd get there ahead of her like last year. But I'd have to tell her sometime.

Late evening I near the clearing where we've made camp. I hear voices: Joshua and Kim, but I ain't used to them talking to each other. They stop before I can tell what they're saying, and when I get to the clearing they sit next to each other, smoking. Damn if Kim ain't smoking a shuck.

"How's the herd?" she asks.

"Snaky." They got beans still warm so I open some rum and set to. "We can scare them toward the house, bring those boys out. Guards same place as before, plus two night herders."

"Night herders on a ranch?"

I shrug. "Five guards."

Kim glances at Joshua. Truth is, I can't figure it.

Never does get proper dark, what with the full moon. Kim takes her slicker and sets off on foot to spook the herd, which has bedded down quiet. Joshua and I lead Kim's and our horses to some brush a hundred yards back of the corral. The remuda's in the corral and a guard on them too. He don't look too interested in the stock, but then I expect nighthawking ain't his regular job: he wears two six-shooters and holds a rifle across his lap, rides in slow circles round the corral, which keeps the horses agitated. Bastard ought to let them sleep.

Away off I hear the night herders singing. Kim has to wait until they're on opposite sides of the herd, at nine o'clock and three o'clock to her twelve. Then she'll try to spook a couple of steers so the night herders don't know right off a person done it.

Joshua and I creep wide around the corral. That guard's all eyes and ain't but low scattered brush to protect us. We move when he faces the other way, stop crouched over when he comes back around. We're in plain view but still enough to look like brush and shadow. We feel him look our way but ain't no click of a gun, no falter in his horse's slow walk. He continues around and we move again.

We come alongside the house. Windows glow with the last redness of a fire. We see five forms curled under blankets; the rest must be in the barn. We can't tell one from the next but I'd lay odds one's

Sheila and another's Sheriff. Ryan too, maybe, but I don't tell Joshua that. If it ain't true, no point in saying I thought otherwise, and if it is, well, then it is.

We crouch, waiting. We can smell the herd, that thick odor of hide and dung. Any other night I'd love the smell of a sleeping herd. We keep perfectly silent, even our breathing is silent. We both hold rifles and our six-shooters hang loaded at our hips. Winchester rifle can shoot seventeen rounds without reloading, which makes twenty-three each with the Colt.

God, but it is quiet. You can hardly hear the herd breathe, and them night herders' singing comes and goes on the breeze. Even the birds and coyotes done shut up, and I wish they'd talk so the guards would believe this is just another night.

I creep to the front corner of the house and peer quickly around it. Damn if they even got the front door guarded. Guess no rustler trusts another, can't say I blame them. I creep back and signal Joshua about the guard.

He nods. In the moonlight his black eyes glint. For a minute I feel cold, like everyone and everything I ever knew up and vanished and I float with my guns in complete silent blackness.

Then a rumble shudders up through the ground, like the whole earth aims to crack open. Far off someone hollers, "Stompede!"

Shouts come from inside the barn. Horses snort and metal rings clank on saddles. The rumble gets louder.

I hear Sheriff say, "What the fuck?" inside the cabin. I risk a glance through the window as we move to the front. They're all getting up, but I can't stop to see who's who.

Joshua runs around the front and smashes the guard in the side of the head with his rifle butt. The guard drops without a whimper, but it don't matter because now 12,000 hooves beating the earth pound your ears near deaf.

The stuff swings into view, running toward the bobwire fence at the near edge of the pasture.

Joshua hurries back to me. The front door opens and Sheriff and Sheila bolt out.

"Sheriff!" Joshua screams over the din.

Sheriff wheels on him, rifle ready. Joshua pulls the trigger, you barely hear the report, and Sheriff lurches sideways. Sheila and a couple others turn on us and start firing. We shoot back, hit two men, duck behind the corner of the house. The nighthawk races from the back corral toward us, raises his rifle. Comes at a dead run. I aim and fire and he falls, catches his foot in the stirrup. The horse zigzags, the nighthawk bounces over cactus and rock. Blood leaves a black trail in the moonlight.

I fire another shot around the corner, hit one of the men. He ain't dead. He shoots back. They all shoot back.

The other men spill out of the barn, most mounted. They heard the shots and the cattle and look confused as hell.

"Over here!" someone screams. Sheila.

Joshua hears too, pokes around the house and shoots, but the others are back in the house.

"Look out!" hollers Joshua.

I dive.

Joshua shoots above me at the window.

The herd leaders get caught in the bobwire. It cuts them to ribbons, stops them, but the rest climb over and head for the house. The riders wheel their horses and ride for the herd. They sure ain't cowhands.

Someone races around the barn and I raise my gun. Joshua pushes the barrel away: Kim. She drops next to us, breathing hard.

"Got Sheriff," I holler.

She nods, checks her Spencer.

The herd and the rustlers meet. The herd splits and goes around the rustlers, who look stupid as hell in the middle of it. The herd reaches the house and barn, splits and goes around, passes close enough for us to touch. The heat from them burns our faces, the dust chokes us. We snatch our bandanas, cover our noses and mouths. The roar goes inside our heads and pounds our skulls. Huge horns sweep over us, close to the house, some brushing the house. We crouch low.

The rustlers spin their mounts and take after the herd and the roar sweeps into the night like a passing train. Dust settles on our hats and clothes.

We move quietly toward the front of the house to finish the job. Maybe it's done already, who knows. I'm leading. I get to the corner. No one's out front. Then I hear a shout and spin around.

"Kim!" Joshua yells.

I try to raise my rifle. My arms move so slow. I see Kim turn, lift her gun even slower. I see Ryan Buckley on the other side of her, his rifle lined on her, his finger squeezing the trigger. Joshua lowers his shoulder and thrusts it into Kim. Kim flies to the side, slowly, too slowly. I see a flame at the end of Ryan's gun and my own gun booms. I see another flame from Ryan's gun. I fire again. Ryan goes down.

Lead tears my thigh from behind and I turn, pull the trigger. Sheila falls.

Silence. The deadest, most Godawful silence, silence like that black nothing, and I feel so cold. I stare down at Sheila as she dies. I watch her squirm. She works her mouth like she wants to say something, then spits. I do not want to turn around. I point my rifle at Sheila and shoot her again and she dies.

But I have to turn around. I have to. I hear movement behind me. Turn around. I can't. I let my rifle drop: it adds a puff of dust to the dust from the herd, which is still settling. You can hear it settle, I swear you can.

FOURTEEN

Mercedes lives in a room at the back of a cantina in a Mexican town called San Fernando. Behind the room is a boulder. In the morning the sun comes across the Gulf of Mexico to Refugio County, Texas, where I was born and raised, and where I murdered my father because he murdered my brother. My brother's name was Mick. He was older than me but slow. Never talked much. My father drank all the time and beat Mick for everything. So I killed my father and my mother shot me in the shoulder, and I ran off and worked up north before coming back to Texas. I am a wanted man, by the law anyway.

I came back but hell I never should have. Now the sun blazes across Refugio, across Live Oak County south of San Antone, across where the Buckley outfit used to run wet stock and sell out their friends. Across Rancho Renova and into San Fernando, with the monastery on the hill and the cantina and the jacales of the vaqueros who work for Don Vicente Renova. If you sit on that boulder behind the cantina in the morning the sun reaches under your hat brim and hits you in the face and makes you look old. You stay there long enough, the sun swings to the front of the cantina and leaves you in shadow. Then it gets dark and starts over the next morning.

Kim comes out and tries to tie a bandage around my thigh and I tell her to go away. She stands in front of me holding the bandage so it hangs to the dust from her hand. She walks off. Inside she tells Mercedes she don't care if I bleed to death. I won't bleed to death: stopped bleeding at Buckley's.

The rustlers came back. We shot about four of them, but there were too many more and we had to run. We had to leave the body behind. I don't know how long ago that happened: years, maybe.

The sun shines in my eyes, shimmers in the air above the prairie. Swings overhead and around the world and back again. In the shimmer I see a man walk toward me: tall, lean, dark, but all I see is the outline, black in the shimmering air with the sun behind. Walking slow, to shimmer and vanish, to return, to vanish. I sit on the boulder and lean against the cantina, and when Mercedes brings me a bottle I drink. But when she brings food I send her away. She brings cigarros and I smoke. But no food. She touches my shoulder and goes inside. And it is night.

I watch the moon rise and the stars come out. Sallow moon at first, then cold and hard and white, a chunk of ice. Stars are cold too, like you fired a gun into a block of ice and it shattered. Mercedes brings a blanket to me, but I send her away.

"You have to give this up," she says.

No I don't. Hell with her. She goes inside. Next morning the sun comes up and makes me look old all over again. How many times can one man look old? Sun swings overhead and down the other side. Mercedes brings a bottle and some beans. I eat the beans and drink the whiskey. She brings a blanket. I stand and take the blanket and start walking east.

"Where are you going?" Mercedes asks.

"Renova."

I find Kim asleep in the room where Don Vicente kept me after the snakes. It is late and no one knows I'm here. I close the door to the room where Kim sleeps and stand over her, holding the blanket. My leg ain't so bad, I don't even limp. Kim opens her eyes.

I unfasten my spurs and pull off my boots, then my pants and shirt and underwear. I throw the covers off Kim and see she is naked. The moonlight makes a rectangle on the floor near the bed, and in its faint reflected glow Kim's small boyish body looks silver. She holds out her hand but I don't take it. I lie next to her and cover us with Mercedes' blanket. I trace my fingers over her whole body and kiss her everywhere. Finally I part her legs and she opens for me and I push into her. I push and touch and kiss until she is satisfied, and then I lie still until she sleeps.

I will leave before she wakes up. If she grieves, the grief won't last. If you think about it, nothing really lasts.

PART TWO

FIFTEEN

Sometimes when I ride up Juniper Canyon I see myself coming, like I'm two of the same man, one crouched on the South Rim of the Chisos at the head of the canyon, watching with mirror eyes, and the other riding in. The canyon slopes sharply down from the South Rim, which is brushy on top. Grass covers the walls, except at the very top where they are craggy and straight up. The slopes sweep from the rock heights to the canyon floor, the earth under grass and scattered brush forms ridges like muscles under a man's forearm.

I crouch high up and watch my other self. He looks tiny in that canyon, just him on a sorrel horse. His head is bowed so I can't see his face. I don't want to see his face. I gaze beyond him to where the canyon fans into the head of a low rise, and after that the river winds and the Sierra del Carmen slices the sky. I have the uneasy feeling that I am looking deep into myself. I get up and stretch, turn and walk into the brush, away from the canyon.

Then I am in my own body again. Funny how being alone can play with your mind. Never took to being alone, now I think about it. Always had folks around, even if they wasn't always the best company. But then, what's good company anyway; I sure ain't.

My sorrel snorts and I scan the South Rim.

"Smell a cat?" I say.

He tosses his head. The string behind me dances, skittish. All except Joshua's horse: he can run like hell and cut any ladino from the brush, but besides that he's the quietest damn horse I ever knew. Best trained, too. Joshua could sure train a horse.

I realize we've stopped, so I nudge the sorrel and he walks on. After awhile we round that last hill and the cabin comes into view, dark and dead. Off to the side the wood-fenced corral stands empty, and beyond that a wood cross juts out of the dry ground. The stones are still piled on the grave, but that makes sense because we only buried him a few weeks ago. Seems longer.

It's already the shank of the afternoon and I'm tired. Inside the cabin I rustle some beans and tomatoes and wash it down with a half bottle of Jack's. I sit in front of the fire a long time, drinking and thinking pretty much of nothing. Halfway to morning I take my blankets outside. The dry grass crackles under my back and the air is thin and brittle. I watch the stars shift. In the corral the horse snorts; probably that cat prowls nearby.

Joshua used to stay awake all night, sit by the fire and watch the flames go to embers and finally ash. I close my eyes and sleep.

Red must have moved to higher ground, because only a pair of white-tailed deer hang around the pasture where I left him. I stand in the pasture with the hackamore on my shoulder and whistle for him, and the whistle echoes off the sandstone rim of the canyon.

I remount the sorrel and wind up the back wall toward the South Rim. Sun's up full, parching. Might as well light the grass on fire. Prickly pear still hold plenty of water, but this will be a dry year, you can feel it already.

The sorrel tops the rim and I point him through the low brush toward the Basin, a spring-fed bowl high in the Chisos. The grass is always green there and the air never gets real warm. A rough ride will leave man and horse breathless that high up.

The sorrel and I stop at the edge of the Basin. On the other side a few bighorn sheep graze. They raise their heads, make sure we're just another animal, resume grazing. A breeze ruffles the thick green grass, rippling to the center of the bowl.

Red stands alone out there. He sniffs the breeze, eyes me with his head high, swishes his tail. I get off the sorrel, walk slowly toward Red. He watches me come. I stop fifteen feet from him and feel my shoulders slump, like I'm too beat to walk the rest. He eyes me a long time, then walks up and shoves my shoulder with his muzzle. I rub his neck, lean against his withers.

"Wanna stay up here?" I ask him. "Whole damn canyon's drying out, but you knew that."

I pat him again on the neck, remount the sorrel, and ride out of the Basin, through the brush and down into the canyon. Red watches us go through black-rimmed eyes in his fine Arabian face.

Back at the cabin I rustle some chuck and wash it down, fall asleep under the stars toward morning. Seems like a long time passes and life goes on like that, if you could call it life. Sometimes I hunt, shoot a deer, and eat that for a few days. Once I come across a bull calf in the brush. It lies so still I near trip over it. I raise the Winchester, take aim. Veal ain't bad meat, though I prefer full-growed ladino. My finger curls round the trigger, but hell with it, I lower the gun and start to walk off. I ain't took but two steps when a ladina cow crashes through the brush toward me. She has horns set frontward for hooking and blood in her wild eyes.

I dive sideways, roll, come up. She runs past, wheels, charges. I dive, roll. She wheels again, jerks her head to show those huge, forward-hooking horns, charges. Damn. I raise the gun, look down the barrel to between her eyes. She's ten feet away tearing through the brush when I pull the trigger. She drops in front of me.

That calf never moves. I stand over him wondering if I ought to shoot him too, but a man can only eat so much beef. I butcher the cow, take as much as will keep.

"*Adiós, ladino,*" I say to the calf. I walk off and he starts bawling.

Some days I ride to the Basin to see Red, but I never bring him down. The Rio Grande will have narrowed by now, the banks will stink with slime. The grass has turned brown and brittle so you hate to walk on it. You think that maybe if you tread careful you won't break it and it will green up at the next rain. But the sky goes to copper and the wind brings dust, not rain.

Sometime in midsummer I have a birthday. I turn twenty-seven and feel old. I got no idea which date is which, but the heat and the sun tell me when midsummer comes and goes. I feel about as parched as Juniper Canyon. The springs retreat underground and the sorrel and I have to go up the slopes to rock tinajas for water. We haul it back to the cabin. Even the supply of liquor dwindles, but I might rather do without than ride to Presidio for more.

Some days all I do is sit out front of the cabin scratching my beard, shaggy now, and drawing on whatever bottle come to hand first when I woke up. Usually I ain't full drunk, just half there. Some days I get up earlier than others and the sun shines in my face and I know I look about a hundred years old. Once I go inside after the guitar, bring it out and pluck a few notes. Sounds out of place, though, like if an opera suddenly opened in the canyon, so I put it back in the cabin and leave it alone.

I think three months have passed and I ain't seen a human soul. Rainy season ought to come along but the prickly pear take to dying and the happiest thought I have all summer, maybe one of the only thoughts, is that the rustlers took all the stock and I ain't got to listen to them bawl. I sit out front of the cabin and listen to my beard as I scratch it. Sounds like the grass crackling underfoot. Then I listen to the last of the liquor slosh from the bottle to my mouth. And I wonder what the hell I'll do with no more liquor.

Guess I better head to Presidio, but not right off. I take to walking around the canyon. I walk near two days straight and feel sick by the end. Got to get to Presidio for liquor. But I feel sick.

I try to saddle the sorrel. He gives me trouble. I feel powerful sick. My arms itch, like spiders crawling up and down them, tarantulas with them hairy legs, tickling, making me itch. I take to stumbling around the canyon again. Next I know I'm up at the Basin, standing in the middle. Red eyes me from the side.

"Go to Presidio," I tell him.

He tosses his long black mane. His forelock falls over his black-rimmed eyes.

"Go to Presidiohhhhh!" I scream. Then I just scream, no words, no words I ever heard anyway. But I ain't heard words in so long maybe I forget. I set cross-legged in the middle of the Basin, at the bottom of the bowl. I scratch my arms and my beard. Hot as hell, even here. Sun shines copper, sky is a copper bowl upside down over the Basin's green bowl. Hot as hell. I take off my undershirt; ain't worn a buckskin shirt in months. Sit in the sun and it turns my skin red. Lie down, grass cools my back, sun bakes my belly. Hell with you, sun.

Shadow. Open your eyes. Big shadow, sun's gone black.

"Hi, Red."

Nudges me, tries to turn me over.

"Go away, Red."

Nudges me. Shove him away. Stops nudging me but keeps blocking the sun.

"Thanks, Red."

I lie there for days, I think. All of life seems like forever. My beard itches so I take out my knife and cut most of it off. Don't stop itching. Weren't the long part that itched. Get up and go to the cabin. Got to shave.

The Basin looks bright. Every blade of grass stands out bright green against the others. Sun sparkles on spring-fed streams. Red glistens: blackest points, reddest coat. Grass smells clean, moist: no dust. Peaks stand out the color of fresh-cut oak against the sky. Blue sky, not copper. I never seen such a clear world. Hold my hands in front of me and they stand out sharp against any background. Take a step forward: boot on the grass makes a small matting sound but it's so clear. The whole world looks, smells, sounds so clear. I am sober.

I could panic, I expect to. I expect to jump on Red and run him without saddle or bridle all the way to Presidio: whiskey, tequila, rum, whatever the hell they have to offer. Anything. But I don't. I only want to shave.

I locate my undershirt, head for the South Rim on foot, carrying the shirt.

I climb through the brush, which scratches my sunburn, and I ain't felt much of anything in so long that the sharpness of scratching feels like a whole new sensation, like I added to my five senses, or grew them bigger. I climb down the back wall. So much happens around me: every bush, every rock, every blade of grass hits every sense and I feel like I took a drug to make it stand out. I could panic, but truth is I'm kind of amazed and numb, though numb seems wrong in the face of all this action. Nothing ever moves, not even a breeze, but it all seems sharp, cutting sharp.

When the cabin comes into view I stop short: a black horse stands in the corral with the sorrel. He wears a saddle and bridle, but don't look lathered from here. Joshua rode a black horse. But we killed that horse. Don Vicente's houseboys carried me into the hacienda and behind us that horse quivered and fell over dead. We rode him to death. Joshua never said a word about it, but we did.

Anyone in the cabin can see me easy. If he's looking he could've picked me off already. If it's a he. Could be Kim, if she got a saddle and a new horse. But it ain't: no way she'd follow me here.

Well, hell, I walk around front of the cabin and wait for someone to come out.

"Anyone in there?"

After a minute the rawhide door flap opens and a big man with thick bowlegs, slicked blond hair, and an ivory-handled Colt comes out.

"Who the hell are you?" I ask.

"I'm looking for Peter Jack Costello," he says. Got kind of a thin voice for such a big man. Yankee, by his accent. "You him?"

"What if I was?"

"I'm a Texas Ranger. Got a warrant for his arrest. Murder charge." He looks close at me. "You fit the description. Sure you aren't him?"

This seems kind of funny to me, so I chuckle. First I've laughed at all since forever, and maybe this ain't the time, but truth is it's damn good having someone here.

"You want some chuck?" I ask. "Long as y'all're here you might as well eat."

He shrugs. "Sure. Where've you been, anyway? I got here three days ago."

"Ain't rightly your concern, I reckon. But, hell, I been up at the Basin. You know the Basin?"

"Sure."

He's a little jumpy, like he can't figure me out. Reckon he can't. Texas Ranger, hell. That's all I need.

"I heard of Pete Costello," I say, shaving. "Most folks down here have. But I ain't him."

"Who are you?"

"Who are *you*?"

He kind of shrugs. I got to chuckle. He's some off his guard.

"Clayton," he says. "Henry Clayton."

"Never heard of you. I'm Pete Jackson."

"Well, I've heard of you. Reckon you and Costello might be one and the same?"

I laugh outright, wipe up from shaving. I left the mustache. "If we are you're in a heap of trouble. I'm going after meat; you don't trust me, come along. Deer okay?"

He comes along and I shoot a deer. We roast the meat outside, the night being warm, and sit at the fire eating. We don't talk when we eat.

"Sorry I got no liquor," I say after.

He fetches some from his saddlebags and we drink up, polish it off, and he brings a second bottle. He has one of them flushed complexions makes him look like a drinking man.

"How'd you get to be a Ranger?"

"Same as you get to be anything," he says, but no more. I'd lay money he had a scrape up north and come down here to start over. Old enough to have fought in the War, the bastard.

"How long you been trailing Costello?"

"Not long. Couple of months. We got a tip he was involved in a massacre over toward Carrizo Springs. Apache named Joshua Deuel got killed, along with a couple other outlaws named Ryan Buckley and Sheriff. Others, too." He looks pretty close at me, but not too close with all that tequila. I don't let nothing slip.

"Costello got away," I say for him.

"Along with another person, a boy by some accounts, a girl by others. We figure it was Bellaca, the rustler."

"Heard of her too."

He nods slowly. "I'd like to find out what really happened at that ranch. Lots of area ranchers would: Buckley was supposed to run a big rustling outfit. Costello might've done us a favor, but he's still wanted."

"Righto," I say, and figure it's about time to turn in.

Next morning I wake up pretty early and the Ranger still sleeps, though he likely sleeps pretty light. I make coffee and he wakes up.

"Well," he says over coffee, "I guess I better take you in."

"Yeah?"

"Sure. You want to come peaceably?"

"Not really. How you plan on doing it?"

He shrugs. "One way or another. Not here, that's for sure."

"No, wouldn't be real smart to try it here. You really think I'm Pete Costello?"

"Sure."

"Huh. Maybe I ought to try and shoot you."

"Maybe."

But I don't. He rides off later that morning, down the canyon, and I feel that same relief I felt when the El Paso deputy released Kim and me from jail. I just ain't in the mood to shoot a Ranger.

After Clayton leaves I ride to the Basin, put the hackamore on Red, and switch the saddle from the sorrel. I ride down the other side of the Chisos, leading the sorrel, and head north. Along the way I cover my tracks.

SIXTEEN

I trail up the Pecos, through the desert hills where if there is any water it's gone so alkali it'll wring your belly, across the staked plains, high and flat except for sudden sharp chasms; run out of cash and sell the sorrel to a cowhand off the Bar BAD in Scurry County. So Red and I ride along, money from the sorrel buys whiskey to ease the drought, beans and whatever; hell with a hotel room, I sleep outside and Red lives off grass like he pretty much always done: rustling his own feed makes a horse tougher, more savvy; sleeping outside lets a man breathe easier.

Sleep under the stars on the prairie and you got the whole world and all God's heaven, if you want it. Even if you want it, you likely don't know what to do with it, but you got it anyway and sure beats four walls and a roof.

On the way to Sutherland's Circle S Ranch we cross the Red River, looks like a wide, wet, brick-color slab dragged behind someone's horse. Driftwood stuck high in the trees tells you the river ain't always so sullen, but now quicksand sucks at Red's ankles and the water hardly seems to move. Bars of earth divide it into channels; sit your horse long enough and watch the water tear down the bars and build a whole new set. Funny, because the water barely seems to move at all.

Several days north of the Red we sight Mobeetie, a Panhandle town used to be headquarters for buffalo hunters. Still a rough town, right at the northwest corner of the Circle S: nine saloons and plenty of girls on Feather Hill. Take your pick. Nine ain't so many saloons, but inside the men are rough. Buffalo ran out and the hunters mostly went back to whatever they done before, drinking and outlawing and making trouble. Some drifted north and others took up ranching, but the rough ones hung on here.

Mobeetie also serves Fort Elliot and the area ranches; I reckon folks have a regular hog-killing time come Saturday night. Or before.

You see Mobeetie first on the horizon: some trees, buildings, not much, but stands out stark against the dusty blue sky with white puffy clouds that never rain, not this year. Grass crunches under Red's hooves going in, air smells mostly like dust, except if you think about it hard enough you can probably smell the liquor from those nine saloons, maybe even pick up a whiff of perfume from Feather Hill. Then you look along the horizon and see the whirlwinds of dust and you know all you can smell is dust because that's all there is: Mobeetie has to be a mirage.

The time since I left Juniper kind of runs together. I ride toward Mobeetie across flat, treeless land. I ride through the Circle S but it looks like the antelope own it, or the coyotes. Or the wolves. Longhorns in their many dull colors speckle the range but you see nary a fence nor rider. Headquarters are east of where I ride now, which puts them southeast of Mobeetie. I'll ride down tomorrow, see Rafaela. Hell.

I heard Garth Sutherland runs near 70,000 head of cattle on 800,000 acres. Never heard he give up running the ranch, but he has. Now I know it.

But first Mobeetie.

You ride on and see it ain't a mirage. Something catches your eye to the right, you look and a band of antelope bounds across the prairie between you and the town. When they get directly between, the air shimmers and the antelope balloon to huge leaping creatures, eight times the size of the town, which squats small and stark between long sinuous legs. The air shimmers again, the antelope shrink and disappear. Mobeetie remains.

I step into the tub with a splash, sink into the scalding water and a layer of trail dust forms on the top. I have a cigarro clenched in my teeth and the smoke goes into my lungs and scours the dust. I cough and lean my head against the back of the tub. After a minute a Chinese girl tiptoes in and asks if I want her to wash me. She's about the size of Kim, only smaller in the wrists and rounder in the face. She has a fixed smile that makes her eyes go away.

"No," I say. "Thanks."

She bows and leaves and I lean my head back again. I close my eyes and see those antelope, bigger than the Chisos. A sizzling sound wakes me from dozing: I dropped the cigarro in the water. Water's all trail grime.

I soap up, call for fresh water. The Chinese girl hauls in a big pot, awful big for someone so small. I help her though she tries to make me stay put. I get out of the bath, help her dump the water, pour in the new. When I finish she don't want me to pay the man who runs the place. He says something ugly to her and takes my money and I leave. Reckon he'll slap her around some. I head for one of the saloons.

"Beer," I tell the bartender. "No, whiskey." He starts to pour. "Double."

"Two bits," he says. He is an old man, stooped. Sharp eyes pretend not to check me over.

A pair of bristly looking hombres arm wrestle at a table on one side of the saloon, which ain't more'n a shack with tables, bar, mirror behind the bar, pictures of fleshy naked women. The wrestlers grunt and strain, you can tell they're red-faced even in this gloom and sure smell their sweat.

"Bet?" the bartender asks me.

"Bottle on the red shirt."

The red shirt wins and the bartender clunks a bottle of whiskey on the bar. The wrestlers breathe hard, pound the table and the bartender draws them a couple of beers. I finish the double and pour another. It's the shank of the afternoon already. Whiskey tastes like horse piss.

"Got any chuck?" I ask the bartender. I can smell steak, but chances are the man lives out back and that's his dinner. He disappears through a rawhide flap.

I hear a woman holler and pretty soon the bartender comes back with a tin plate of fried steak and onions. Brings one for himself too, and we set to eating. Sizzling in the back resumes. The steak is tough and near raw; I seen beef hurt worse than this get better but I don't let on, just spear the red chunks with the fork and drown them with whiskey. I share the bottle with the bartender and the bristly hombres take up wrestling again.

"Bet?" I ask the old man.

He shakes his head and wipes steak juice off his droopy mustache. Damn if he don't nearly grin.

Well, I have to see Rafaela and better to get it over with. But, hell, I'd sure rather go somewhere else: no joy telling a woman her husband's dead.

Funny about Rafaela, though. I seen her at Doan's two and three years ago, picked up her letter last year. Something cool about that woman, cool and smug, if you could call it smug. I don't know, I never understood. Andy talked about her off and on, nothing much, hinted that she might be old man Sutherland's daughter, and sure enough when I seen her she has plenty of white blood. But still.

Well, I got to tell her and no help for it. I been in Mobeetie near twenty-four hours, already run into some boys from the Circle S in that bar. They came in after good dark, stood down the bar from where I and the old bartender was playing penny ante blackjack and took to whispering like a couple of girls in church. Finally one of them came up to me and asked if I weren't Pete Jackson, trail boss. Sure, I told him, and he went on about how another hand said I weren't on the trail this year and how he himself raised a glass with me in Dodge in '84. Dodge is usually a blur for me, so I guess he's right. Truth is I ain't sure I cotton to the notion of everybody in the whole damn state knowing me ten miles off, and maybe I ought to just light out for Alberta and the hell with telling Rafaela: she'll never find out, never get hurt, just wonder. Bound to happen with a man like Andy, that one day he'd disappear.

I asked the cowhand if Rafaela still cooks for the Circle S. He traded looks with his friend, kind of smiled.

"Yeah," he said. "Sure, she cooks. Listen, you looking for work?"

"No. Just Rafaela."

Well, she is beautiful, no two ways about it, Negro or not. Half-Negro. I'll just saunter over to that old livery and saddle Red and ride to headquarters. Righto. But first I'll eat some breakfast.

The old bartender brings four eggs over easy and fried potatoes and bacon for each of us.

"I went up the trail once," he tells me.

"Yeah? Circle S?"

He nods and licks egg yolk off his long droopy mustache. "Others too. Went up near every year since '67. Circle S was my last, went up with Jess Arnt in '83. Rode point, too. So y'all're a trail boss."

The last egg slips along my throat. The curtain to the back opens and a scrawny old woman brings a basket of cornbread.

"This here's Pete Jackson," the bartender tells her. "Trail boss for Renova, that big spread in Chihuahua." It's Coahila but I don't let on. He ain't told me either of their names.

"Y'all cook right well, ma'am," I tell the old lady. She don't crack a smile, makes her scrawny way to the other room.

"Man could do a lot worse than to sign on with the Circle S," says the bartender. "Whole lot worse. Course, old man Garth's crazy as a horse on locoweed, but that place runs itself. Seems to, anyway."

He wolfs a piece of cornbread, which is hard and grainy as clay soil in a drought. Guess I better head southeast. No help for it.

When you ride near Circle S headquarters you'd think you was anywhere but a giant ranch. Wood-frame buildings hug the ground, you don't even know you're there until the gate, which sits on the flat prairie with no fence on either side, all by itself, and those low buildings, dark wood, beyond. Short grass country here, but you'd think the grass got real tall and the buildings sank into it: like you can only see the tops of them. But it just ain't so. Barn, cookshack, bunkhouse, a few corrals close in, main house rambles. The gate says Circle S and you half expect the place to pop up when you ride through but only the distant whirlwinds rise higher than the horizon, and not much at that.

Red sidesteps after we pass the gate. I pat him on the neck and speak low but he's skittery as hell.

Closer in you can see every nail been hammered careful, place is built solid, just don't stand out. A board-floor porch stretches along the front of the main house. Chairs of longhorn and rawhide and drumlike tables with rawhide tops back up to the wood outer walls of the one-level house.

I climb off Red, wrap a rein around the hitch rail, and step onto the deep, dim porch. Someone watches me through the window in the front door. Rafaela. She opens the door. I take off my hat and hold it in both hands, and the edges of the brim feel frayed against my fingertips.

Rafaela's stare reaches all the way inside me from eyes green as pines on a mountainside, green below a high coffee-color forehead, green above broad high cheekbones, green to bring the parched prairie to life, or suck all the life from it and keep it for themselves.

"Thank you for coming."

"Joshua's dead too," I say.

"And Ryan and Sheriff."

"You knew?"

"Not about Andy." She says his name like she might say lamp or wood or glass, but all I can hear is the sound of shovels slicing earth.

"Will you come in?" She opens the door and walks in ahead of me, tall, haughty, and that's when I notice she wears a dress of white lace and green fabric that shimmers with every movement, makes her appear to move even when she stands still. I never seen a ranch cook wear such a dress, and sure as hell never any Negro.

"Have a seat," she says in her low smooth voice, spreading one long-fingered coffee-color hand toward a stuffed chair. Inside the place has a rough comfortable look, fits with the easy smoothing of browns on the prairie: deep-cushion chairs at one end of the big center room, a long pine table in the middle, black bear rugs on the floor, quilts tossed over the chairs. Rafaela in her shimmery dress looks like an emerald dropped into the middle of a cow camp.

"Would you like a drink?" she offers. She barely has any drawl, sounds like she been north for finishing. Andy told me once she reads all the time, likes Shakespeare best. My ma used to keep a book by Shakespeare but I never seen her open it, only dust it off every day along with all the other books; in this center room of Garth Sutherland's low solid ranch house one whole wall is books, floor to ceiling, and when Rafaela fetches my drink I notice they don't show a speck of dust.

She hands me the drink, Jack Daniel's from the taste. I ain't set down yet, I'm standing in front of the books.

Rafaela smiles coolly, pulls a volume down with one long-fingered hand: *Romeo and Juliet.*

"This is not his best," she tells me, and opens it without cracking the spine. None of the books have cracked spines. She fans the pages, replaces the book, pulls another and reads.

> 'Tis better to be vile than vile esteemed
> When not to be receives reproach of being,
> And the just pleasure lost, which is so deemed
> Not by our feeling, but by others' seeing.
> For why should others' false adulterate eyes
> Give salutation to my sportive blood?
> Or on my frailties why are frailer spies,
> Which in their wills count bad what I think good?
> No, I am that I am, and they that level
> At my abuses reckon up their own;
> I may be straight though they themselves be bevel.
> By their rank thoughts my deeds must not be shown,
>   Unless this general evil they maintain:
>   All men are bad and in their badness reign.

I swallow a mouthful of whiskey.

Rafaela sits in a chair by the window, still holding the book. Not much light gets through the window because the porch is so deep. The whole room seems dim and the fireplace is cold. Rafaela gazes out the window, across the droughted prairie. Beyond the porch the prairie is so light it hurts your eyes; you'd never think brown grass could shine so.

I stand by the window, drinking, looking out, holding my glass, which is near empty.

"Dry this year," says Rafaela. "Look at the grass."

Garth Sutherland turns up after dark and Rafaela has supper ready for him. He is an old, old man, or looks like one: sparse white hair, filmy blue eyes, hooked nose, deep vertical lines on either side of thin, sucked-in lips. I guess he just got off a horse and he's bowlegged as hell, but looks like riding would rattle every bone. He shambles through the front door and sees me sitting by the window. Rafaela's in the kitchen, which is part of this main room. The old man shambles over to me and I stand. Rafaela walks from the kitchen, unties her white apron.

"This is Pete Jackson, Garth."

"Pete Jackson," he says, kind of high and broken, like he has a hard time forcing the words. "Pete Jackson, trail boss. We bought our seed stock from Don Vicente Renova six years ago. You drive that herd, Mr. Jackson?"

"No. I only started three years ago."

He turns to Rafaela, pats her arm, and kisses her on the cheek. Then he shakes my hand, lets go quickly. "Glad to meet you, Pete Jackson. How about some libations, Rafaela? Mr. Jackson here must be parched. Parched out on those prairies, right, Mr. Jackson?"

"Right."

He peers carefully at me, tries to size me up; maybe once he knew how to know folks, maybe that's how he got his power, but now those old eyes and likely the vision behind them are faded as a waterless sky.

"I heard you missed the drive this year," he says. "You stay on Renova?"

Rafaela brings the drinks.

"Part of the summer. I had a run-in with a nest of baby rattlers."

The old man chuckles but only with his voice. His face always seems to move but never smiles. He throws back his drink. Rafaela left the bottle so he pours more, throws that back too, belches.

"Got to have my before supper drink," he says with a hand on his hollowed middle. He still wears his leggins and hat and dust covers all his clothes. Every time he moves it rises in tiny puffs that remind me of the whirlwinds on the horizon.

"Near half that Renova seed herd was black cattle," he says. "Damn snaky bunch, and light, but now we've got the strongest, meanest beeves on the Panhandle. You sure you didn't bring us that herd six years ago? Well, I never seen bulls like those blacks. Spend better than half their time fighting, wonder they ever got around to making calves. But they did." He pours another drink and one for me. "Drink up, Mr. Jackson. Call me Garth; call you Pete? No need for all this formality.

"Listen, you're a long way from home. Miss the trail enough to come up without a herd? Looking for work? Ezra and me been riding end to end of that prairie today, dry as a whore at 6:00 A.M. No damn rain since winter, seems like. So what brings you up here? Brought us new stock, maybe a present from Don Vicente Renova? Hell, I'd sure admire to meet that old boy. Cigar?"

I take one, light his and mine.

"How's the drought in the south?" he asks. "Worse, likely. Prickly pear dried yet? You know, we really ought to put a few windmills on this spread. J. A.'s got some, hear the water's sweet as cognac. Heh, heh, won't make you feel as sweet, though. Give me whiskey, though, before and after dinner. Nothing like good whiskey, eh, Mr. Jackson, Pete?

"Bet y'all missed the trail this year. I went up, always do, wouldn't miss it for the world. Stompedes and all. Can't sleep summer nights without hearing 'Little Joe the Wrangler,' get Rafaela to sing it for me here sometimes. Went up with one of Robert's herds.

Robert's my second boy, drover, buys from me, good arrangement. Ezra, my first, he manages the place.

"So what brings you north, Pete? Drought too bad in the south? Looking for work? Seems Ezra could use an extra hand for roundup; we're about to start fall roundup, you know. Plenty of stock this year, only sent a third as much as last year north, expect Renova did the same. Prices can't touch last year's. Robert got to Dodge with one herd and the buyer pulled out on him. Crooked deal anyway; we didn't know it, no way to know it. Ever had that happen, Pete? I expect everyone has."

He stops. You can hear Rafaela stir something, you can hear the fire she built in the wall-sized fireplace. Mostly, you can hear yourself think, finally. Garth Sutherland sips his fourth whiskey and stares out the window, only the window is black panes with black night beyond, and he stares at himself. Don't seem to see, though. Sips more whiskey.

"Why did you come here?" he asks after a spell.

"To tell Rafaela her husband died."

He nods slowly and looks right at me the way Rafaela done when I first got here. "I knew that," he says.

Garth Sutherland and his oldest son Ezra want me to work around headquarters through the winter, then Robert wants me to boss a herd come spring. I never figured to stop here more'n a day, two at the most, and I don't want the company of wintering at a ranch.

Garth Sutherland talks near all the time, then he falls silent and it's like you ain't there. Ezra talks when Garth don't. They kind of trade off. Robert never says a word, runs around in a three-piece suit with a gold watch and chain and makes like he runs the whole ranching business. Anyone in ranching knows he loads his chuck wagons with cornmeal and not much else, don't pay too good, and don't know enough to give the Indians wohaw when they ask for it. Lots of stompedes on Robert Sutherland's drives; Indians get some riled when you refuse to pay the wohaw toll. That bartender says you can do worse than to drive with Robert Sutherland, but he's old and misses the trail.

Now I been here three days and damn if I ain't taking on a few chores, drinking with the hands after supper, setting up for fall roundup. Gets to me not to pay my way, but hell, I'd rather just leave.

"'Bout time I headed on," I tell old man Garth. Rafaela and he and I are eating breakfast.

"Naw," he says. "Whyn't y'all stay here? Plenty of work. Where you headed, anyway? North? Hell with that. Stay here. Roundup starts this week. Best if you stick around. Some of these hands're a might green, couldn't hurt to have someone like you around. Seems—"

"I really better head out."

"Perhaps you could work at the northeast line camp," says Rafaela.

Garth looks at her and at me. That's the first suggestion for running the Circle S I've heard her make, but from her tone it's the latest in a long line.

"It will be a bad winter," she says cool and low. "You can feel it and the animals know. The cattle from farther north will drift onto our range and we'll have a hard time keeping enough grass for our own."

Garth says nothing, slurps his coffee, stares off somewhere like he give up his throne and his soul, like an empty old man.

"The only fence on this ranch," Rafaela says, "runs along the eastern border, separating us from the Indian Territory. The North Fork of the Red forms the northern border, and where those borders meet there is a line shack. There are probably some squatters in the area, but as long as they leave enough milk for the calves we let them stay."

Garth nods faintly. "I was a squatter once."

"Maybe you'll take a herd in the spring," says Rafaela.

"Maybe." I feel right bad for old man Garth Sutherland, and spring's a long way off.

SEVENTEEN

I figure finding a line shack on the prairie ought to be easy; land stretches all around, sometimes in a little rise but mostly flat. Horizon marks the only change west, south, and east; trees mark the North Fork breaks, and besides that it's short brown grass, maybe some antelope, longhorns grazing here and there in small bunches, far apart; no fences except that one on the east border, running straight as a railroad track as far south as you can see and north into the trees: two strands of bobwire strung along a row of poles, Texas on one side, Indian Territory on the other, no difference between them and no end of either in sight.

But you'd never see that line shack unless you knew it was there: it's a dugout at the edge of the trees, barely above the ground, and grass like all the other grass grows on the roof. A little chimney sticks about as high as the grass would in a good year, higher than the grass this year.

This ain't a line camp by any stretch, just a dugout in the middle of a whole Godforsaken lot of nothing: no corrals, no stables, and sure as hell no people.

"Sorry, Red," I say.

Besides Red I brung two more horses, solid mounts already shaggy with winter coats, plus two pack mules. I'll build a small corral in the trees behind the dugout.

This camp ain't been used in years, you can tell. I get off Red and walk around, and sure enough you can see where a corral was some time back. I'd bet someone built this shack and the corral before the Circle S took over, probably a lone squatter who thought he'd make a go of it. Indians got him, most likely. I look again at the endless straight fence. I never seen such a fence in my life; if it weren't there you'd never know Texans live here and Indians on the other side. No one in sight now anyway, except me.

I open the half-rotted wood trapdoor and descend the old ladder. Got to watch them wood rungs, some snap in two soon as my boot touches them. I light a match to make sure I ain't got company: all clear. Place is dingy as hell and damp. Got a rough table with three legs and the fourth corner resting on a barrel. Must be a well outside somewhere, maybe in the trees. A piece of rawhide stretches between poles sunk in the earth floor for the bed. The fireplace covers one wall; dirt and God knows what else clogs the chimney.

Clumping noises tell me one of the horses is walking on the roof. The beams hold but some earth shakes loose, sifts to the floor. I hear Red nicker, sounds muffled. You'd never hear anyone coming from far off or even close in. No wonder that squatter is gone.

There ain't a whole lot to do alone in a line shack, or what there is don't take a whole lot of time. I get the chimney unclogged and the shack aired and dried. At least the trees give plenty of wood, and driftwood from the riverside burns right nice. Old man Garth stocked me with liquor, mostly whiskey and rum, and coffee for the morning. I unload all that and everything else, chop down trees, split logs, build a wood corral, turn the animals out. None of it takes much time, the days sidle by slow, the nights inch along with muffled coyote cries and deeper howls of lobo wolves. Reckon I'll hunt wolves and mend that fence most of the time: Circle S offers a bounty for wolf pelts, like most spreads up here.

Every day I chop more wood, pile it for winter. Set a log on a big old stump, heft the axe, cleave the log. Loud crack breaks the prairie silence, I'd bet you could hear it for miles. But the prairie ain't quite silent: always the wind blows, you can hear it through the grass, riffling the dryness, brushing the blades against one another, millions of blades. And through the trees, you can hear it through the trees, rustling leaves dried red and brown with autumn, plucking them loose, floating them to the ground, lifting them in flurries that whisper.

Always on the prairie you have the wind, it dries your skin to leather, makes you squint so you get white lines at the corners of your eyes no matter how young. You can always tell folks who live on the prairie: they squint even indoors, even when the sun ain't no more; they always stay prairie folks, they stand at a fence like this one and gaze along it and squint to try to see where it ends, and when they see it goes clear over the horizon they squint harder, and if they're real lucky it ends inside their mind. But that takes a powerful dose of luck.

Sometimes as the sun starts to sink I set out walking along that fence, here on the Texas side. Point-toed boots ain't the best for walking but I like the sound of the grass underfoot. I hold one hand over the bobwire, skim along it, barely touching, pricking a little. I hold a cigarro in the other hand. On my right the sun blows up redly, the clouds glow, antelope dart in front of the sunset, the prairie makes them huge. The sun and the antelope rush at me, growing. I look east, across the fence, and in the deepening blue of dusk an old bull buffalo lifts his shaggy head and bellows, far off and small. No one answers.

So I turn around and stroll back toward the dugout, light another cigarro, think of the whiskey waiting underground to warm my belly and maybe my soul. The chimney that rises just above the grass gives no smoke, looks cold, like an empty tin can left there by a drifter passing through, but close to the dugout the breeze brings the scent of chopped wood.

I check the horses and mules, descend into the dugout, light a kerosene lantern and a fire, put out the lantern and the aroma of kerosene strengthens. I drink and cook a small meal: fried beef, potatoes, tomatoes from a can, cornbread from cornmeal and tallow. This is not only one night, this is many nights, though sometimes I ain't hungry or ambitious and rip loose jerked beef with my teeth and gnaw on that. Whiskey helps, or rum or tequila. But tequila gives a good, powerful happy boost and I like the other better. And that buffalo moans many nights, along through the fall.

One night along past dusk I walk back from down the fence, moving slow, watching the paleness of my hand over the bobwire, when off east a dark mass catches my eye. I keep moving, watching sideways, holding my head so it appears I'm looking at the fence. The mass gets larger real slow and by the time I've covered another mile or so five Indians meet me at the fence: three bucks and a couple of squaws, Comanches from the looks, on foot.

"Howdy," I say.

Their eyes glisten white, the rest of their features are dark and blurred. The moon ain't up yet.

"You got some beef," says one of the bucks. "You got smoke. Maybe whiskey."

"I got smoke," I say and hand them five cigarros. Old man Garth stocked me with enough cigarros to last until the prairie goes to dust. I give them a match and they light up.

"You got beef," the buck says again.

"No. Not now. I ate it all and no more to kill." I sweep an arm to indicate the range. "No more on this range. Maybe later, not now. Look around: no beef."

The bucks nod slow to themselves. Hell with them: if there were stock near here they'd beef it themselves. And as for whiskey, well, that's mine for now. Unless they get ugly about it. Or unless they know how to play cards.

"You play poker?" I ask.

One of the bucks breaks a grin. The others nod solemnly. The squaws trade quick words in their language.

"Sure, we play," says one of the solemn bucks, "if you got whiskey."

"All right, but you have to win it. Got money?"

"No money. We win."

I laugh and even them solemn bucks smile. The squaws look at me narrow-eyed and smug.

We all climb into the dugout. I light a lantern and they set around the table, the squaws too. I bet they're fair players. No stakes, not even the whiskey; we'll use pebbles. I uncork the first bottle, draw long on it, pass it, build a fire while they drink.

Indians smell different from white folks, stronger maybe, though we probably smell as strong to them. The three Circle S horses danced when we got to the dugout; I could hear them whinny, but not Red. Red got no cause to fear Indians, and he knows some of the scent from Joshua. These ain't Apaches, though, and sure as hell not French-Canadian.

The fire gets to roaring, puts a glow on the Comanches' bronze skin and black hair. They have broad faces, heavy features, high cheekbones, flat mouths. The bucks are naked to the waist though it's cool out and the nights have gone right chilly. One of the bucks has a big lump on the side of his neck and holds his head tilted. He's the one who grinned; he's smaller than the others, as small as the women, and some older though not by much. They're all probably about my age, but so different from white folks you can't say exactly. Not that it matters.

"I got some beans and a little jerky left," I tell them. "Want supper?"

They go on playing while I rustle the chuck. Beans sizzle in the pan over the fire, heavy knife hacks off chunks of jerky. I serve it all and they deal me back into the game. Damn if the squaws don't win most hands, and the bucks don't even care: too busy drinking. Finally the one with the lump on his neck drops out. We each have our own bottle by now except the squaws, who stopped drinking. The other two bucks pull out and me too, so we sit with our feet stuck toward the fire so the whiskey warms our bellies and the fire warms our feet.

The squaws play on, cackling at each other now and then, and though I can't tell what they say I can guess. Sometimes they laugh, sometimes they bitch. I figure they play at who can cheat best.

Two of the bucks snore loud enough to stop the river and the third stares into the fire. I got a bottle of whiskey by the neck and my toes toasty warm and my face hot and dry like it gets near a good big fire, and those women cackling behind me. But then one of the women shrieks and jumps up, knocks her chair over. The other jumps up. This happens behind me; I'm too lazy to turn my head. I hear a slap. Another chair falls over, near on top of me. I hear a rustle and a couple of grunts.

The buck with the lump on his neck groans, rolls over, gets up. I hear him bark something in his language. I hear a fist thud on flesh, then footsteps on a ladder. Cold air tumbles into the room, the door closes. The buck lies back down in front of the fire.

"Women," he says.

EIGHTEEN

The trees in the river bottom come bare and you can see the water beyond. The North Fork can swell to a hundred yards here or run shallow and narrow, like this year. Sometimes I sit for hours on the bank and watch it roll. It always rolls, and I wonder where all that water comes from with this drought. The grass beyond the trees has turned sparse and sharp as needles; stock have already drifted into the breaks for better forage.

The air turns chilly, even under the sun, and you can feel that north wind weave through the trees to breathe across the dugout roof. If I let the fire go out too far before dawn the wind creeps down the chimney and turns the room clammy so I wake up aching and cold. Been throwed from horses enough times that my joints complain something awful about moist cold.

But I pull on my trousers and leggins, boots and so forth, climb stiffly up the ladder, stretch and watch the sun come up. My fingers turn blue but I light a cigarro, and my breath looks as white as the smoke, white like crystals riding the morning air. I squint over that fence at the sun, shift my feet, and rub my palms together. The sky brightens with day, the sun glints off frost that turns the grass silver. I go inside, build a fire, fry bacon and biscuits, sometimes beef if I've rode west and slaughtered one, sometimes deer, sometimes just bacon. And coffee.

So now it's November, I think. Every few days I saddle Red and ride farther south along that endless fence to check for rustlers and such, but the fence holds up fine. Also we ride west through the trees along the bottom. We see bear and deer and all kinds of critters. Or we ride due west, cover maybe fifty miles, sleep under the stars, cover fifty miles back by a different route. Red has a bushy winter coat and the way that wind whips in from the west I wish for a buffalo robe. Hell, I'm too lazy for that.

But one night the old buffalo bull across the fence sets to bellering louder than ever. I can even hear him in the dugout: I lie on my back on the rawhide bed, the fire crackles quietly, the wind whistles across the brittle brown grass and the buffalo moans over it until just listening makes me shiver. The wind slips down the chimney and the fire swells, the room brightens then dims again, and when the fire swells the shadows do too. And that old buffalo keeps right on bellering, the most mournful sound you ever heard, like someone tore out his soul and blew it across the prairie, and if he calls loud and long enough it will hear and return, or at least the one who tore it out will never forget what he done.

Well, hell, I can't sleep with that racket. I throw off the covers, pull on my clothes, shove a new load into the Winchester, and climb the ladder. Maybe I'll fix the broken rungs one of these days, now I skip them. When I poke my head above the trapdoor frosty air turns my mustache near to ice. My breath comes white in the moonlight. Ain't a cloud in the starry sky and the moon so bright you can see the whole prairie clear to the horizon. With the trees at your back it's like a great stage and the stars the audience. That endless fence stretches south, two thin black lines on a row of black posts.

I climb all the way out and shut the trapdoor. That old buffalo bull stands right on the other side of the fence so the bobwire touches his heavy brown coat. Either he wants to push the fence over or he thinks it's his only friend. Or he hates it and has the idea if he hollers loud enough it will go away.

Beyond the buffalo I see smaller dark forms: lobo wolves. They wait for the old creature to weaken, they've probably waited many a night. I raise the rifle and sight along it at the wolves, but they stay out of range.

That buffalo bellows so deep you expect his big head to swell and shrink with each blast.

"You make a hell of a racket," I say, and the words sound harsh and sharp in the cold clear air.

The old buffalo bull swings his head in my direction and surveys me from little dark eyes that seem lost in his huge head. He opens his mouth and bellows again, louder, loud enough to wake all of Texas. One of the wolves sets on his haunches, raises his head and howls. The others patter around some more, then do likewise. I stand on top of the dugout holding the rifle and the metal stock feels near froze to my palm and fingers. I blow on my other hand to warm it but the only way to get warm out here is to have a buffalo robe.

The chorus of buffalo and wolves goes on, gives me a mind to sing. So I set in with "Utah Carl," about the fellow who gives his life to save the boss's daughter from a stompede. No stompedes here; ground's froze like glass and a stompede would likely shatter it. That buffalo and the wolves and I sing for God knows how long, and as I sing I walk slow toward the big brown hulking creature, raising my rifle. My boots crunch the earth and I think maybe it will shatter from just me.

Thirty feet from the buffalo I stop walking and singing. He stops bellering and stares at me like a wounded man who loves you and hates you for what you are about to do. The wolves howl louder, or maybe it only seems that way. The stars seem to sing a chorus of their own, and as I squeeze the trigger I swear one of them streaks to the horizon.

The wolves fall silent at the shot. The buffalo crumples to his knees, rolls sideways, shoves the last air from his lungs in a great relieved sigh.

I climb through the fence, draw my Bowie knife, set to skinning the dead beast. He smells something fierce, a rotting smell like he's been dead a long time. But his body is warm, and when I slice him open steam rises to mix with my breath. I skin him, take what meat I can eat, hang the hide to dry, leave the rest for the wolves, and go to bed and sleep.

After dawn those wolves still gorge themselves. I shoot three and the other two run off. That's bounty on three wolves and God knows how many calves saved: it will be a rough winter and the wolves I don't shoot will eat their fill of Circle S stock. All that's by way of justifying killing wolves while they eat a breakfast I killed for them. And what do I really care about Circle S stock, except old man Garth pays me to keep it alive and give me enough cigarros and whiskey to last until spring. Then Rafaela wants me to trail a herd north. Hell with her, hell with Circle S stock. I skin the wolves.

Buzzards circle overhead, drop as I walk away carrying the bloody pelts. Buzzards'll eat the wolves, who ate the buffalo, and I'll stay warm in a buffalo robe and wolf gloves, and the buzzards will die someday and end the chain, because no one eats buzzard, unless maybe the earth. Yeah, I reckon those gangly old black birds go to dust and the grass grows from them, and that means I walk on buzzard and Red munches buzzard when he grazes.

I hang the wolf pelts from trees near the buffalo hide, which has froze solid. Now the sun starts to thaw it but the morning sun is thin and weak, the sky pale, the prairie faded. The air goes in and out of my lungs thinly, weakly, like it ain't full awake yet.

"You eat buzzard, Red?" I ask him after that. He tosses his black mane, flinches his blazing red chestnut hide. I throw the blanket across his back, the saddle over it, cinch the saddle tight, bridle him with the hackamore. Never have used a bit on this horse. Don't need spurs neither, but hell I feel naked without spurs, sometimes more than without a six-shooter. Ain't shot that Colt in months but I'd walk tilted without it.

I ride through the trees to the river and turn east at the bank. I ride several miles downstream, into Indian Territory. The long fence ends where the riverbank would be in a wetter year, where it was the year they built the fence, I guess. Or maybe they wanted to leave space between the end of the fence and the water. So I ride into Indian Territory and no sign of cattle, Circle S or other. I turn around, ride west. Well back onto Circle S range, I can see through a break in the trees north across the river to the horizon. Land looks the same on that side as on this except that I see a lone longhorn walking this way.

The longhorn plods south, so deliberate and slow it looks like you wound it up and set it to walking. It picks up one foot, sets it down, picks up another, sets it down. And so on. It is still far off, on the horizon, too far to tell its sex or brand. I hook one leg over the pommel of my saddle and watch that longhorn. No others follow but they will: we will have a bad winter and the cattle know it; the drift has already started and I can nearly smell that longhorn on the wind that will soon sweep down from the north.

I unhook my leg from the pommel, ride west. There are no more breaks in the trees but you can feel the drift on the other side, surging slowly and gently against the trees, against the river, against the Circle S boundary, onto Circle S grass, grazing across it, thousands of cattle, grazing over the Circle S to the Red River, some going on, most stopping in the wooded breaks north of the red bluff banks and red slab of water, staring dully, hungrily at the frozen slab, frozen to pink the color of a pale sunrise, frozen like dried blood on a dried, frigid range.

Then the cattle will lower their heads under the weight of heavy horns and turn their haunches to the whistling blue northers, and the horns will feel heavier and heavier until they can't hold them up any longer. Then their heads will droop and they will fall, and the buzzards will come if they ain't froze too, and in the spring the bone-littered prairie will be made of buzzard for Red to graze. Red and the other survivors.

So you peer through the trees on the north bank of the North Fork of the Red River on a raw cloudy November day, and you know what is to come. You take comfort in knowing because later, if you're lucky, you'll grow old and sit by the fire thawing your joints, puffing a cigarro and swirling the last of the whiskey in your tin cup, and tell the young hands about the winter the cattle drifted south and the buzzards feasted. You take comfort because it's only one winter and it ain't your damn ranch anyway and whatever makes good telling ought to make good living. Only when the wind whistles through the trees and flaps the brim of your hat you ain't so sure.

When Red and I swing back by that same open spot on the south bank I see the longhorn is a steer, a pale red lineback with corkscrew horns near six feet across. More cattle have drifted over the horizon behind him, not too many yet, but every second another speck pops over. But one of them specks ain't a cow, it's a man on a horse and coming in from the northeast rather than over the horizon. I sit still while he comes on at an easy lope. Red pricks his ears forward, grinds his teeth. I pat him on the neck.

"Company, Red."

NINETEEN

The man rides to the edge of the sluggish river, splashes in a short way, waves his hand and halloes. I hallo back. He don't seem inclined to cross any further so I urge Red into the chill water. Red don't mind too much, prances a bit but trots across. I raise my feet to keep them dry; water ain't deep.

The man wears range clothing: leggins, boots, spurs, canvas coat, beat-up hat. He's young, younger than me, fair complected, copper-color hair, wide-set hazel eyes, long face ends in a pointed chin. Long nose, wide mouth, kind of large teeth. His skin is reddish and blotched the way some fair folks get outdoors. He carries a coiled bullwhip and wears no gun.

"Name's Mallory Bledsoe." He holds out a big bony-knuckled hand. Looks like a farmer's hand with plow callouses; he sounds like a Yankee, though with a bit of a drawl. Wide grin, but hollow.

"Pete Jackson," I say, and shake his big bony-knuckled hand. "Y'all ride this range?"

"My wife and I have a place a few miles downstream, in the trees. You?"

"I'm riding line for the Circle S. Dugout's over yonder, on the border. Near the fence."

He nods slowly and his hazel eyes take on a funny shine. His pale blotchy skin stretches taut across his nose, making a pearly part on the bridge.

"That's some fence," he says, and his old brown horse shifts under him. "How many miles long you figure it is?"

I shrug. "However many it takes to make the Red River. It runs the whole way down. I don't know how many miles."

"I've never seen such a fence." He lifts his hat to scratch his head. His copper hair is thin and wispy with hardly any on top. "Listen," he says, "maybe you'd like to meet my wife, Sarah. I'm sure she'd like to have company, and to cook for someone besides me. Maybe you'd like to come for dinner. The cabin's only a few miles downstream, like I said before. Maybe you'd enjoy meeting her."

"I'd enjoy some cooking 'sides my own."

He grins that hollow grin and we set off at a lope. Red seems excited about stepping on new ground, cold wind don't pester him a bit, though I wish I had that robe already. My blood must've thinned in the South.

Mallory Bledsoe's cabin pops over the horizon soon enough; God knows you can see everything out here, no place to hide, may be good for me to have that dugout. Next to the cabin is a larger building, a barn. Neither is real big, both stand out dark against the dust-color grass and the bare trees behind. The cabin backs into the trees. Out front a corral holds what appear to be two mules. Smoke coils thinly from the cabin chimney.

We drop to a trot and I feel her watching us: narrowed eyes, wet hands dried hastily on an apron. At the corral Mallory Bledsoe reaches from on his horse to unlatch the gate, we ride in and dismount. I can't figure why we put the horses here when the barn would be warmer, but hell, it don't matter. The saddles creak as we pull them off and our spurs clank as we walk to the cabin.

"My wife Sarah's inside cooking dinner," says Mallory Bledsoe. "She'll be glad to have company, like I said before."

The door to the cabin opens and Sarah Bledsoe steps aside to let us pass.

"Afternoon," I say, and touch the brim of my hat. We put our saddles in a corner and I can't figure why we brung them in here instead of putting them in the barn.

Well, Sarah Bledsoe has them narrow eyes all right and her hands are red, likely from hot water, so I reckon she was drying them on her apron. Apron ain't tied in the back, just hung over her neck and front: she's pregnant and looks near due. Her face is some puffy the way I seen other women get in that condition, but the rest of her is right sinewy and she carries herself like that baby ain't even there, maybe even like none of us is there. She's tall, long-boned, like her husband, not what I'd call pretty though she inclines you toward looking twice. She wears hair the color of a dark bay horse, pulled straight back from a high forehead into a bun large enough to tell you that hair'd hang past her waist if she let it down.

Her skin is browned and damn if she don't look ten years older than her husband, though I'd bet she ain't over twenty-five. And she does have them narrowed eyes, watches me from behind them; they are opaque pale gray and I never seen eyes like that before, I reckon I'd see them even if I closed my own and blew out all the lights.

Mallory Bledsoe's tone changes when he talks to his wife, goes kind of hard and flat and businesslike.

"Sarah, this is Pete Jackson. He's come for dinner."

"How do you do, Mr. Jackson?" She offers a reddened hand.

"Just fine, Mrs. Bledsoe." I hold her hand for a second. It feels near as hot as that water must've been. I let go and she rests it on her swelled belly, which balloons toward me. I get a sudden urge for a drink but neither of them offers.

"Our baby is due next month," says Mallory Bledsoe, "before Christmas."

Sarah and I stand where we shook hands, that belly still juts toward me, like a big iron ball set between us. She ain't took those narrowed eyes off me since I got here, ain't even blinked, seems like.

"What's for dinner, Sarah?" asks Mallory Bledsoe. His voice is so flat you could deal a game of poker on it.

Sarah Bledsoe steps away from me, lets go with that stare. I feel like she was holding me a few feet up and dropped me.

"Venison stew."

She returns to her cookfire, lifts the lid to a big black dutch oven. Steam swirls around her head. She stirs the stew with a long wood spoon. She moves like thick smooth liquid, like good brandy, you don't see her move, she's graceful, she moves but you don't see it, she's one place then another, then she'll freeze, stand so still, grip you with those eyes, with that stillness.

Now she straightens from leaning over the fire, straightens and turns and looks at me looking at her, smiles, smiles with her mouth, with the fluid movements of her sinewy body, movements you feel but never see, movements that swirl around you while the eyes hold you in place.

God, I'd kill for a drink.

"Won't you sit down?" she says.

Mallory Bledsoe claps me on the back. I near belt him one I'm so surprised: he ain't the type. He hauls a chair from the table for me, another for himself.

"Do we have any milk left?" he asks. "Would you like some, Mr. Jackson?"

"No, thanks."

"I realize most cowmen don't like milk, or don't drink it in any case, but it's really very good for you. A man could do much worse than to have a cup or two each day. Certainly it's preferable to the cloudiness brought on by liquor. I find the amount of liquor consumed by Westerners appalling, though you may disagree. In fact, I expect you may enjoy a tug or two on the bottle yourself. Well, we keep no liquor here; nothing will turn a man faster than an excess of liquor."

Sarah sets a tin cup of milk before her husband but he leaves it on the table, wraps his big bony hand around it, studies it while Sarah studies me. Then he looks up suddenly at Sarah, she switches her stare to him but the expression stays: no fear, no hatred, no guilt.

Mallory Bledsoe stands, hauls back his hand and slaps her across the face. You can tell she saw it coming but she never flinches, only her head turns sideways and her brown cheek goes red, and for a second her left hand grips the back of a chair, her knuckles whiten.

I am standing and not knowing when I stood. My hand grips my gun halfway out of the holster.

"There is a devil loose in this house," says Mallory Bledsoe, working his mouth, clenching his fists, but his tone is cool, flat, businesslike; he states a damn fact, no more.

"And the Lord will smite that devil," he says, "before it smites us. The Lord will smite it and the Lord has instruments for meting His punishment."

I let the gun slip back to the bottom of its holster. So far I am biting my tongue so hard it's near bit off.

"I better be going," I say when I can trust myself not to say worse.

Mallory Bledsoe smiles hollow-like, a grin in a skull. "Please stay. There is no reason for you to go. Please sit down."

I look at Sarah. Her cheek is still red.

"Stay," she says evenly. "We would like to hear about your trail drives. You are a trail boss, aren't you? I think I've heard of you, if you're the same Pete Jackson. Don't you recognize his name, Mallory?"

Bledsoe goes on with that hollow grin. "I must confess I don't. Where did you trail this year? Dodge? Montana?"

"Nowhere. I got snakebit and stayed down south."

"Oh," says Sarah and for a minute I'd swear I can see inside. Then she serves dinner and we set to. After we start on seconds she finally joins us, and only then can you tell that baby makes it a little hard to get around.

"We're from Ohio," Mallory Bledsoe tells me. "Actually, both of our families started in Pennsylvania, near Pittsburgh, but emigrated to Ohio when we were young. Sarah's family had already settled when mine arrived. Her father was a Methodist minister."

"Yes," says Sarah.

"We came out here two years ago," says Mallory. "Leaflets, you know, land of opportunity. When I first saw the plains they seemed endless, big enough for all men and the beasts they tend."

"Only in wet years," I say.

He smiles, hollow.

"This your first year on the North Fork?" I ask.

He nods. "We started with some cattle from the Crisswell, just above here. Herefords. They say that's the breed of the future, that the longhorn's days are ending. I suppose you've always worked longhorns?"

"Snaky bunch, but they'll do."

"So do you think their days are on the wane?"

I shrug, swallow a mouthful of venison stew. Truth is it's all right but harder to swallow with no liquor. "Truth is," I say, "I don't give it much thought."

Sarah watches me, I can feel it. Bledsoe gets up and puts a log on the fire. Sarah rests one hand on the table and lifts the fingers a little. I figure I better go, probably should've gone before, or never come in the first place. But no help for it now, no way I could've known, you can't know a thing until it happens.

"Excuse me," I say, "but that was fine chuck and I got a range to ride."

Outside the clouds have dropped so low you almost need to

duck, and the wind whistles out of the north. Temperature has dropped a good twenty degrees while I been at Bledsoes' and I want to get that buffalo hide made into a robe right quick. This norther hits full force I won't have nothing else to do but sit by the fire and stitch that robe and pretend not to think about Sarah and Mallory Bledsoe. Think about the cows and the prairie and wash it down with old man Garth's whiskey while the cattle drift south.

But I got to wonder if Mallory Bledsoe done a bit of mavericking. I reckon if his Lord don't rule against a deed he'd consider it fair play, but you never can tell. Folks are funny that way and no help for it; you just never can tell.

TWENTY

It snows for three days, and not even December yet. Smoke from the fireplace layers the dugout with a film of ash; every now and then I open the hatch to let in fresh air and clear away the snow. God knows I'd hate to get trapped down here. Fire don't make much light, feels like night all the time, drive you a little loco after a spell.

On the morning of the third day I have to step outside for more than a minute: a man can only stay in so long. The wind swirls the snow around me, white spots make the whole world, the snow is two feet deep but tailing off. I stray from the dugout, into the trees. Surprising how gentle the wind blows but this ain't a blizzard, only a long storm. So I walk through the trees and feel right warm, always feel warmer in the snow though I ain't seen a whole lot of it since drifting back to Texas.

I scoop a palmful, pack it into a hard ball, fling it at a tree. It shatters. I pack another, shatter it. After awhile my hand is red from the freezing wetness and bits of snow melt between my fingers, drip to the white ground. My feet get cold so I go back inside, pull off my boots, roll up that buffalo hide, lay against it with my feet to the fire and a tin cup of Jack Daniel's on my belly. Just like I used to lay on the bear rug at Tridente, and then sometimes Kim would curl next to me with her head on my chest and my arm around her small tight-muscled body, body like a boy's except the breasts and other female parts, body like no other for making love.

We made pretty good love, Kim and I, and though I don't think of her much I have to wonder who makes love to her now. I ain't been with any woman since I left her, you know, but ain't nothing to do with her or me, just the way of it. Just the way.

Next morning you can tell the snow stopped, even inside with no windows. I must've fell asleep in the afternoon and slept through, because the hearth is gray and dead, cold air slips out of it across my bare feet, numbing them. I can see my breath it's so cold in here, which means the clouds lifted in the night.

So I get up, pull cold socks and colder boots over white-cold feet, rub my hands together, climb the ladder and open the hatch. Sun pours in like a river, spills down the ladder, brightens that old dugout to near cheery. Outside the snow shoots the light every which way, the prairie gleams white as far as you can see and only the upper wire and tops of the posts of that endless fence poke above the white. I cover my eyes, give them a chance to adjust. Bright makes my head pound, but sharp, not sick, sharp like knives glinting in the sun.

I go back inside and make coffee, take a cupful and a hunk of jerked beef and trudge toward the corral. I can see the gray and paint and blazing red chestnut hides through the trees, and the dark brown of the mules. Trees cast long blue shadows. My boots crush the snow, sink deep, and the air has that clean white scent like always after a snowstorm, that scent that backs up every other scent, so you're kind of bombarded but not overwhelmed because everything smells different from everything else. Looks different, too: see the way them horses and mules stand out against the white ground and white on dark tree branches.

South Texas could do with more snow, and Renova gets none.

I climb onto the corral fence and sit drinking coffee, gnawing beef, watching the horses. My feet rest on the rail but with the snow drifted against the fence I can't see them. The animals have pawed to the grass, and it hits me that this is the first break in the drought and that's why the air smells so clean and good.

"What do you think, Red?"

He looks up from grazing, sniffs the breeze, tosses his black mane.

"Me too," I say.

The horses graze, then suddenly one lifts his head and prances or even bucks a little, like some feller prodded him with a stick. Then he grazes again, then frisks, like he's two beasts. I watch their antics for a spell, you can tell they like this weather right enough. Finally I fetch the bridle and saddle, climb on the gray, and set out to check the cattle drift. I have to shovel snow away from the corral gate to get it open.

The North Fork ain't froze and longhorns of every color from grulla to dun to pale red wander through the trees on the other side and dot the white plain beyond. Most of them graze, having nosed through the powdery snow, and they seem pretty content on the north bank. That'll end with the next chill wind: they'll cross that river and march to the Red, and they'll sweep Mallory Bledsoe's whitefaces along too, until he's got nary a cow on his own range.

I see a few of Bledsoe's mixed with the others, which likely hail from near every spread north of here. Look careful at their brands and dewlaps and you can see some from Wyoming and Colorado, maybe even farther north. This will be a hell of drift before it ends, and I reckon the Circle S will gain its share of mavericks. Maybe Mallory Bledsoe will too; I still have to wonder if he mixes some Circle S stock with those whitefaces. Damn if their bulky brick red bodies don't stand out sore among all them lanky pale longhorns.

Well, as long as the stuff stays on that side of the river, let Mallory Bledsoe worry about it. Maybe then he'll keep his God damn hand off Sarah.

Funny, but I feel kind of like I ought to watch out for her, though nothing about that woman asks for watching out. Just the opposite. Well, I'd rather not think about her anyway, and sure as hell not worry. I have a range to ride and a fence to keep mended, and God knows women are trouble. Hell, I got no more love for women than for anything else, and a good horse fits better under a man than a troublesome woman.

I pat the gray on the neck and let him walk or trot or go however he wants toward the fence. He has a mind of his own today. Every so often he seems to look down for his feet and when he sees them disappear it spooks him into a little run. I laugh and hang on; no way to ride a horse but what the hell, the gray's all right, dapple near sixteen hands, strong, generally well-mannered though he will try for a chunk of your shoulder if he thinks you ain't looking. Probably can't touch Red for speed or quickness but size and strength give him an edge otherwise.

We reach the fence and turn south and the snow has already melted a few inches. You can about hear the ground underneath slurp the moisture, you can almost feel its thanks as the soil darkens and the grass roots fatten and stretch.

The stubby fenceposts stick up dark and there's still only one strand of wire visible. I squint against the bright. We cover several miles. My eyes get used to the glare but I still squint. A bunch more miles and it looks like a break in the fence ahead. Hard to tell with all this white, plays tricks on your eyes, snow could've drifted. We ride closer and sure enough it's more than a mirage.

We come alongside the cut part, only one section between two posts, and no tracks on the snow. Stock passed through before the storm. No way to tell how many head or where they went, but pliers clipped that fence and no reason the stuff would've drifted east, they'll drift south, not east.

Well, I don't want to track through new fallen snow, so I fix the fence and figure to go after them later. If this sun and warmer weather hold the snow will melt in a few days. If not, maybe the rustlers will come back for more.

Turns out the weather don't hold, gets colder and colder until even the air hangs stiff under the cloudless sky with stars too froze to twinkle. I check that cattle drift every day but they look to've froze solid on the north bank. Sit long enough and see them move real sluggish, but usually I don't sit that long. I can't figure how it could be so freezing and so sunny at the same time.

Around supper I sit by the fire and piece together the buffalo robe, then after good dark I ride along the fence, checking for rustlers. The snow gets crusty on top and anyone could hear me coming from miles off, but that's all right, I can hear them better.

By the end of a week I have that robe ready and wolf pelt gloves, so I ride longer at night. The whole prairie glows blue under the moon, you can see where the snow meets the horizon and above it the darker blue sky with pinprick white holes, like a blizzard rages outside the sky but inside the air holds still and silent, except when hoarse wolf howls tunnel through it and coyotes yip beyond. Sometimes it's so still the wolves sound right close, though you know they're far off. Some nights you see them: black shapes dart in twos and threes, or alone, stop to raise their fangs to heaven, swell their throats and howl, and the howl goes into your ears and down your own throat to settle frigid and thrilling in the pit of your stomach.

But no rustlers, only wolves. Now I like the night rides and sleep more through the day. I've never known the plains to have less wind: even cigarro smoke hangs when you blow it out, and the horse's breath stays below his nose as he plods along the fence.

Seems like years with no wind, though only a couple weeks pass, and I guess it's getting on toward Christmas when I finally pick up the rustlers' trail.

TWENTY-ONE

The tracks tell me there are three of them and they made off with forty or more head of cattle. I sit on Red and light a cigarro and stare west, where the tracks come from, and the tracks make a deep wide furrow in the moonlit blue snow.

They cut the fence farther south this time, near twenty miles south of the dugout, and come through here before dawn yesterday, from the looks of the droppings. Appears they were right choosy about the stock: the front hooves left sharper prints, so they're all steers, and big ones from the depth of the prints, probably dress six hundred pounds each if the rustlers work them slow.

It's near dawn, the east sky has started to pale, and by the time I fix that fence and set off, the horizon glows the color of salmon steak above the snow. I could go for any kind of steak right now, beef jerky's damn near froze in my saddlebags and the whiskey with it. Good to have the buffalo robe and wolf gloves.

The tracks bear northeast. I'd lay odds they'll cross the North Fork and sell to a buyer on the other side, so I have to catch them before that unless I want to take on six men instead of three. Ain't decided yet what to do with the three when I catch them.

The land wrinkles into small hills as I ride along. Red's hooves bust through the snow, the crust has got to hurt his ankles but he keeps going. We move slow compared to good weather travel but you can tell from the droppings that we're gaining. The speed these rustlers move those cattle won't dress but five hundred before long: they cover up to twenty miles a day, the fools. Hell, I'll catch them anyway.

By the shank of the afternoon, barely past three this late in the year, the trail is so fresh that steam rises from the droppings, which have melted the snow under them and sunk in. I'm pretty tired, having slept last more than twenty-four hours ago, but no stopping now: Red's ate up near thirty miles and from the tops of the hills you can make out the timber that marks the North Fork. Red has to feel beat but he keeps loping, got the smoothest lope of any horse I've ever rode, you think you move slow but before you know it you've reached wherever you're headed. Any good horse can do that, so can any good man. But you figure it don't generally work out so easy.

Well, we top a low ridge and the next hill after that and as the sunlight flickers a final adios, I sight a curl of smoke rising above the trees against the dusk blue north sky. I swing Red east a quarter mile and ride along the edge of the trees. Pretty soon camp comes into view: three men, three horses, forty-three Circle S Longhorn steers. The men don't have extra mounts.

They've made camp in a little valley with a stream running through to the North Fork. The stream has froze on top but you can see its course by a crease in the snow and the rustlers have dug for water in one part. I take off a wolf glove and reach into my vest pocket under the warm buffalo robe and pull out a cigarro and a match. From the way those rustlers hold their bare hands around them tin coffee cups they feel a hell of a lot colder than I do. I smile at that but ain't no mirth in it: I been so damn cold on the range plenty of times and not made near what these fellows will make off forty-three Circle S beeves, even if they do drive them too hard.

I nudge Red and he walks toward the camp. I take off my other glove and open the buffalo robe so I can reach my six-shooter. When the cigarro gets low I toss it away.

The rustlers hear Red's hooves crunch the snow and two of them rise with their right hands at their hips. One wears his gun way too low and tied down so I ain't worried much about his talent, only his temper. The other stands shorter though both are short and look dark and you can't tell much at a hundred feet. The one in the middle stays hunkered down, and closer in you see he's working his cheek around a chaw and holding his hands in front of him, palms to the fire. He's older, maybe fifty, looks older'n that, gray hair to his shoulders, firelight furrows the creases on his face above a gray beard streaked with black.

The two standing on either side of the old man have to be his sons, though both look half-Mexican and the old man looks Anglo. The taller kid eyes me with a sneer that appears fixed in place; the other watches calmly. The old man don't even glance up until I dismount ten feet in front of him.

"Evening," I say.

None of them replies, except the shorter one coughs deep and wipes his mouth. Then the old man looks up, like he finally finished studying the fire.

"Nice night for a ride," he says, and drenches a coal with dark juice. The coal sizzles, turns the juice to steam. The old man rotates a hunk of spitted meat, probably deer, that cooks above the fire. The coffee pot sits on coals to the side.

I kind of smile. "Mind if I warm my hands?"

Them boys ain't moved a muscle. Now the one who coughed looks at the old man. They're all scruffy but then I'm pretty scruffy myself, bearded now and my hair way below my ears.

"Go ahead," says the old man.

I squat and my knees crack. I hold my hands over the fire, though they ain't especially chilled.

"I got some whiskey," I say.

The old man nods. He never looks me in the eye except that once, when he said about how nice a night it is for a ride.

"Plenty of meat," he says. "Help yourself."

The shorter boy coughs and hunkers down but the other one stays up. They're probably sixteen or so, maybe the taller one is older, maybe eighteen. Lot of boys wear that sneer at eighteen. I go to Red for two bottles of whiskey.

"Nice horse there," the younger boy says, holds a cough. He don't look fevered but that cough come from way down.

"Thanks." I uncork a bottle and hand it to the old man. He pulls deep, wipes his whiskers with the back of his hand. "Here, Caleb." He thrusts the bottle at the taller boy. "These're my sons," he tells me, "Caleb and Tom. I'm Pinto."

"Pete Jackson." I shake his hand, which has knobs around the knuckles and leather for skin. I shake Tom's hand and finally Caleb sits on his saddle on the ground and lets me shake his too, but he keeps that sneer and when I said my name you could see the fire crackle in his dark eyes.

Pinto pulls out a big old Bowie knife and chops a hunk off the spitted meat. He hands the knife around so the boys and I can do likewise. It's deer all right, gamy and tough as an old boot. But, hell, I'm hungry, we're all hungry. We pass the bottle and gorge ourselves, though I let them eat and drink the most, and halfway into the third bottle Tom has gone to yacking between his coughs and Caleb's sneer turns uglier. Pinto ain't no different from two hours ago, still sets and drinks and spits, turns all the rocks around the fire dark tobacco brown.

"Ain't you the Pete Jackson works for Vicente Renova?" asks Tom.

"The same. Cigarro?"

Tom takes one. Caleb declines by lifting his bristly upper lip on one side. He almost looks amusing, but hell I sure don't let on to laugh.

"I God," says Tom, puffing smoke like a prairie fire and coughing. "Why the hell you up here in all this snow?"

I smile and shrug. "Not much to do around Renova in the winter."

"You could always rob a bank or two," says Caleb, low.

Pinto looks at him and then at me, and that's only the second time his fox-smart old stare has come my way.

"A bank?" I say.

"Sure," says Caleb. "You and Chiso Deuel. You remember Chiso, don't you? Half-Apache, used to ride with Ryan Buckley and Sheriff and some nigger. I heard where he used to work for Renova too."

"That so?"

Tom looks a little nervous, looks at his brother. Pinto spits. Tom coughs.

Caleb lifts his lip. "That horse." He juts his chin toward Red, who's still saddled. "That horse come off Renova? I heard the old don raises the finest horseflesh anywhere."

I draw on my cigarro. Whatever this kid wants from me he ain't going to get it.

"Ain't that so, Jackson? Don't the don raise the finest horses?" He stands, walks to Red, tries to put a hand on Red's neck but Red tries to bite him. He raises his hand to slap Red.

"Don't," I say.

He kind of laughs, sidles back to the fire but don't set, snatches the bottle from Tom and tilts it, brings it down and coughs. I notice Pinto looks hard at him. Tom stares off somewhere, working his fingers.

"I bet Chiso Deuel trained that stallion," says Caleb.

I stand up kind of slow. "How about if we lay off Chiso Deuel."

Caleb shrugs. You'd never know he was drunk, it makes him mean but not sloppy.

"What for?" he says. "Because he's dead?"

I got my gun in my hand and jab the barrel hard into his belly and he grunts, and I feel Pinto and Tom rise behind me but I don't move that Colt or look around. I slap Caleb hard across the face with the back of my left hand, slap, not punch, and trade no words. His head jerks sideways and he loses his balance but gets it back. I point the gun at his flat nose and the nostrils go wider and his mouth opens partway and fear leaks through the hate in his black eyes.

He knows who I am and he can see his father over my shoulder and he thinks that gives him the right to hate me for who I am, and right now I'd like to stick that gun straight up one big flared nostril and squeeze the trigger and blow the top of his head to the smoky black sky. Fuck him and the whole world too.

But the gun weighs a ton in my hand and feels as hot as fire.

"You better close your mouth," I say, "before your teeth fall out."

He does, but the sneer returns, distorts his lips, his face, his whole self. I holster the gun and turn around, and Pinto and Tom stare at me and damn if Tom ain't trying to hide a grin. Well, he's drunk. Pinto, he looks pretty cool and solemn, maybe sad, though that's a strong word for it. I can feel Caleb behind me, feel his fear now that I don't see it. He lives on fear. Some folks have nothing else.

Pinto hunkers down and paints a rock with tobacco juice. "Set, boys. Jest set and let's make some peaceable medicine."

"Some folks got funny ideas what peaceable means," says Tom, but he looks at his brother, not me.

"I'm gonna check the herd," says Caleb. "You want to come, Jackson, I'll be waiting."

"I God," says Tom.

"Later." I light another cigarro. I can see I'll get about as much sleep tonight as last night, and that no one except Tom will get drunk enough to make this easy. So I down the half bottle I been wanting all evening anyway and by the end of that I'm tight enough to at least feel all right about reclaiming them damn steers. I guess I do doze off some, but lying on my left side wrapped in the buffalo robe with my right hand wrapped around my six-shooter.

Come dawn I get up and drink coffee while the rustlers rouse the stiff sleepy herd. I never did unsaddle Red, except to rub him down and resaddle him right away, so as the sun shoots gold rays above the east hills I mount and ride to where the rustlers are carajoing at the herd, riding around it, kicking snow to slush.

Caleb notices first when I slide my Winchester from its boot and angle it in their general direction. He drops his hand to his hip. I squeeze the trigger and his six-shooter and holster snap off. The pistol falls deep in the snow and the holster dangles from the thongs around Caleb's leg. His horse dances and rears. I shift the Winchester to my left hand, swing it toward Tom, draw my Colt and point it at Pinto.

"You know," I say, pretty loud because the cattle have took to bawling and pounding their hooves through the crusty snow. "It ain't smart to wear a gun that low. Makes it some hard to reach and mighty bothersome when you're working cattle, whether them cattle belong to you or not.

"Now, I know y'all worked hard to drive these Circle S beeves here, but they're still going right back. So head out due west, follow the river. Don't give me no trouble or I'll drive them myself and leave y'all for the coyotes. Savvy?"

"You don't need us," says Pinto. "You ain't gonna kill us here and ain't turning us in neither."

"Damn straight he ain't," says Caleb, with his horse quieter now.

"Shut up," says Pinto. "Take the fucking beeves. You don't need us."

I chuckle. "Sure I do. I got a warm dugout and plenty to drink and it's lonely as hell on this prairie. 'Sides, look yonder at them clouds. This sunshine ain't for long. Now come on, let's get this stuff moving. Let's go."

Damn if a grin don't sneak through old Pinto's whiskers, and that kid Tom sees it and grins ear to ear. Caleb, well, he sneers. Then he unties his dangling holster, stuffs it in his saddlebag, digs his six-shooter out of the snow and sticks it in his belt. He remounts and rides to Pinto, they exchange words I can't hear, but I got a fair idea Caleb will come along with us. What the hell.

TWENTY-TWO

We drive them stiff sleepy longhorn beeves for three days, due west, and damn if it don't feel nice setting a horse alongside them big swinging horns and listening to them long-tongued critters bawl. Feels right nice, but something eats at me and I can't shake it, something about every damn Texan knowing me before I get to introduce myself. I guess they can recognize Pete Jackson all right, but then you have fellows like Caleb and that Ranger, Henry Clayton, and you got to wonder how many other folks know who I am underneath. But hell, I ain't Peter Jack Costello any more than Pete Jackson, not really, and no cattleman's association or wanted poster can know all of a man. But they can shape his life.

I've drove three years for Rancho Renova, and maybe that's too long, maybe I ought to gone on north or west instead of stopping at Sutherland. Hell, I figured to do just that, but a line job in Texas puts as much distance between a man and the rest of the world as any job anywhere else. Or it should. Now I got three rustlers on their way to Christmas dinner, though Christmas could come today for all I know of the calendar.

I got no love for rustlers, but that old fox Pinto stands life easy enough to suit me and Tom comes off all right too, though that cough will rip him apart sooner or later: he coughs all the time like he don't notice, like he's coughed most of his life, which maybe he has. Coughs right in the middle of a word sometimes, in the middle of a drink, a smoke, and during sleep, coughs and the cough is all of him, all of his life. No help for it, but Caleb ought to cough, not Tom.

Well, two days and we sight the fence stretching from straight ahead, coming out of the trees, to the south and out of sight. Snow done melted enough so you can see both strands of bobwire.

The law calls for a gate every three miles but this fence marks the state boundary and not too many herds nor men need to cross it for reasons acceptable to the law, so old man Garth gets away with hardly any gates at all. We drive the rustled beeves through the northmost gate, near the dugout. I swing the gate shut and latch it and we turn the beeves loose.

"Looks like old man winter rustled a few head himself," says Tom.

"Yeah," I say, "and more to come." West, on the Circle S range, cattle walk south in twos and threes and slow-moving bunches. The sky has gone cloudy now, the snow has took on a grayish cast to match it, and the cattle plod over the gray snow and under the gray sky. They retreat before the winter, but seems they move toward some god or altar or maybe just better feed, rather than away from winter. They don't act like critters ahead of a chase, they don't act like longhorns walking north in the summer; they don't look beat, neither, only like they have no choice, whether they like it or not, so they might as well walk on and not worry about it. That's why you can't stop a drift: it is destiny with a will of its own, and no help for it.

"Be hell come spring," I say.

"Can't stop a drift," says Pinto.

"Got some whitefaces in there," says Caleb, sneering.

Tom coughs.

"Folks across the river run whitefaces."

Pinto spits.

"They'll freeze. Or starve."

"So will the longhorns," says Pinto, looking north. "Bitch of a winter."

"Righto." I unlatch the corral gate and put the horses inside. In the dugout we get a fire roaring. Tom offers to beef a heifer; God knows we have our choice of brands.

"Take one of them whitefaces," I say, and after he shoots one he and I butcher her on the ground, where she fell, and as we slice her open damn if the thought of Sarah Bledsoe don't cross my mind, and damn even more if I feel a hint sorry we killed that heifer.

"Man owns this cow got a pregnant wife," I tell Tom.

"I know." He coughs. Steam from his lungs mixes with that rising from the carcass. "I seen her."

My knife stops slicing, sort of all by itself, then starts again. "What the hell," I say, "we're just saving winter the trouble."

"Yup." He coughs.

We finish butchering and cart the ribs to the dugout to roast.

"That stuff'll walk clear to the Red," says Pinto over dinner.

"I seen brands from Wyoming out there."

"Montana, even."

"Montana, hell," says Caleb.

"Drink?" asks Pinto.

"Sure," I say. He passes it.

"I bet ranching goes belly up this year."

"This year or next."

"You taking a herd north for Sutherland?" Tom asks me.

I shrug.

Pinto kind of grins. "North, hell, take all spring and summer to split that drift. If there's any left."

"They'll be okay," I say. "Breaks on the Red make pretty good shelter. It's the ones stay in the open that'll die. That snow gets good and crusty, no cow's got sense enough to break through."

"Not even a longhorn."

"Sure as hell not a whiteface."

"Woman above the river's about to drop her foal," says Tom.

"That oughtta be inneresting," says Pinto.

Caleb half laughs. He laughs near as ugly as he sneers. Tom coughs hard enough that he gets up and stands coughing over the fireplace.

"You figure it's almost Christmas?" I ask.

"Who knows?" says Pinto.

Tom coughs all night, seems like. Even after drinking I sleep light; I trust Pinto and Tom as well as you can trust a cowhand, but Caleb is trouble. He knows who I am and I bet he ain't told the other two, I bet he wants that reward for himself. I ought to left him behind when I got the bright idea about company for Christmas. He ain't said he knows, but when you see him look at me and then at his father you can tell. The bastard will double-cross his own father and turn me in, you can bet on it.

So I sleep light and as the days go by and the four of us turn back what cattle we can I get some ornery from lack of sleep. We work our butts off trying to turn that drift, though I can only pay those three rustlers with a hint that old man Garth might dole an extra wage, and if he don't they can have the whiskey and a bunch out of them forty-three rustled beeves. Or a bunch, anyway: the forty-three done made for the Red River soon as they crossed the fence.

So here we are working up a sweat and freezing in the river at the same time, and it all seems pretty much a damn fool effort and I even want to agree with Caleb when he says we ought to just build a fence.

I wipe sweat off my face and the thought of that buffalo robe makes me drip: we work in lighter jackets and vests except when the wind blows good, which probably accounts for Tom coughing all night, every night.

"We can't build a fence," I say, "because the cows behind would pile the front ones against the wire and it would rip them to shreds."

"So?" says Caleb. "They ain't your beeves."

"And you ain't no cowman."

"Damn fucking straight." But he keeps working. Sometimes he works harder than the rest of us: works angry, like he festers inside.

One day we hallo Mallory Bledsoe across the river. He don't hear us at first, he's busy cutting his damn whitefaces from the cattle bunched on the bank.

"Hallo, Mallory Bledsoe!" I holler louder and finally he hears. He turns in the saddle, figures out who I am and rides to the water's edge.

"You a father yet?" I call across, over bawling and the crunch of hooves on snow.

"Not yet!"

"She okay?"

"Yeah!" And he goes back to working his whitefaces loose.

The three rustlers and I sit our mounts on the bank, breathing a bit hard from the work. When you set still the wind cuts through you, jacket or not, plays with the brim of your hat, ices your ears and fingers. But we set a spell, catch our breath. Then Tom coughs.

"I'm going across," I say. "Y'all want to keep working these drifters?"

"Sure," says Pinto. "What the hell."

I put Red into the freezing water, gray now like the snow under the clouds. Sun stays hid these days but the clouds seem to forget how to snow. I ride across the shallow river to where Bledsoe hollers at his stuff, lets his old brown horse do the cutting, though he does crack that whip now and again. I have to admit that gotch-eared old gelding works better than he looks. After breaking a young beef loose, Bledsoe rides to me.

"You picked up some new hands," he says, and you can tell he knows what they are.

"You had any trouble with them?" I ask.

"Not yet."

I smile. "They're okay, except the older boy. He's trouble."

Mallory Bledsoe looks at me like I'm trouble. Self-righteous son of a bitch.

"I come to help you cut your cows," I say.

"No need."

I shrug. "This is pretty far from the house."

"No need." But I help him anyway. He works steady and grim, not the best at it but good enough. He pays me no mind, even seems to veer off if we get too close. This work goes fast compared to turning the drift, which is a fool's errand at best, and by late afternoon we have a hundred or more head of Bledsoe stock bunched for the drive toward the cabin.

"I'll take it from here," says Mallory Bledsoe.

Well hell, but I touch my hat and turn toward the river. "Let me know if you need any help," I call over my shoulder. "With that baby and all, you know."

He makes like he ain't heard, pushes his stuff into the dimming east.

"Hell with him, huh Red," I mutter, and splash at a lope to the other side. The rustlers have already quit and headed for the dugout.

The cattle stare dully at me from the north bank and I feel some sorry we drove them there: they'll only cross again. Some of them have crossed every day, and no help for it; they have to wonder why we keep recrossing them, but then again they probably stopped trying to puzzle cow folks a long time ago. Truth is I wouldn't turn them at all if old man Garth weren't paying me for it.

I catch up to the rustlers, who drive a whiteface calf toward the dugout. The calf bawls.

"Let it go," I tell them.

"We're out of beef," says Caleb.

"Just do it."

He reins in his horse and I rein in Red. Pinto and Tom ride on a few paces with the bawling whiteface between them, then they stop and turn in their saddles. The calf goes right on bawling, stands in place and bawls.

"It's only one fucking calf," says Caleb, "and ain't yours neither. Whyn't you lay off this bullshit and leave Bledsoe's wife to Bledsoe?"

"Caleb," says Pinto, low and looking at me. I think he expects me to plug the kid right here, but truth is I ain't got it in me. Truth is all of a damn sudden I'm tired of Mallory Bledsoe and the Circle S and pretty much all of Texas, but specially of thinking about Sarah Bledsoe's swelled belly every time I hear a whiteface bawl, thinking of her so much that Caleb sees it though I ain't said hardly a word.

"Kill the fucking calf," I say, but neither Caleb nor I move. He sets his horse and damn if his sneer ain't gone, but only for an instant. Then that lip lifts on the side and he laughs, ugly.

"Women," he says.

"Righto," I say. "But I'm still going up there."

Pinto shakes his head and spits.

"Why?" says Tom.

I shrug. Red shifts under me and I nudge him forward. We all start moving again, and pretty soon the dugout chimney comes into view.

"When you going?" says Tom.

I turn Red into the corral, slide down, pull off the saddle, curry him nice. We all treat our mounts well.

"Dunno," I say. "Maybe I'll change my mind."

Tom coughs, curries.

"That Bledsoe's pure bastard," says Pinto. "We stopped there for some water and out he comes with that bullwhip coiled in his hand. No gun, no gunbelt. 'Plenty of water in the river,' he says. Pure bastard. We seen the woman watching us from the cabin, skinny but with that rounded belly, standing there in the dim inside like he keeps her locked up."

"He don't," I say. "He can't."

Pinto snorts a laugh, spits. "Come again?"

"She ain't the type."

"She married him."

"She's a preacher's daughter."

"So?" says Caleb.

"Well, they're raised different," I say. "You got to figure it. Feller like Bledsoe all hepped up to move west got to seem right exciting to a preacher's daughter."

"How do you know about that?" asks Tom.

"What, that she's a preacher's kid? Bledsoe told me. Over dinner."

"No, about how one would act. How do you know that?"

I finish currying Red, pat him on the withers and he tries to nip my shoulder.

"Getting cold out here," I say as Caleb butchers the calf. "I'm going inside, start a fire."

"How'd you know?" Tom asks again.

"I don't, but it figures."

He coughs. "I don't think it figures."

I don't think he figures. "What's the difference? You know a preacher's daughter once?"

"I might of. Once."

We climb down the ladder to the cold, damp floor and the odor of mildew and men and old tallow gets in our skin. Tight living for four, I guess, but I've seen worse, we all have. I lay the fire quick, because even the dark smells and the lantern don't cut it so well. The flames kick loose and burn off the dankness but the smells hang on. Then we set the meat in the dutch oven, cut the bad parts off potatoes and onions and add them, and after a spell all you can smell is beef.

"What girl you talking about, Tom?" Caleb prods. "I never seen you with no preacher's daughter."

Pinto stares at the fire, spews tobacco juice into the flames and watches it sizzle. I uncork a bottle and pass it to Tom.

"I guess she were more of a priest's kid," he says, coughing after a slug of bourbon. "Down Yselta way. Coupla years back."

"You was only fourteen and she were a whore's filly," says Caleb.

"Don't make no nevermind, she were a priest's and no whore herself, hell with what her mama done. Her mama were right nice. For a cat. Cats ain't as bad as all that."

"No," I say. "They ain't."

"How'd you know she's a priest's kid?" says Caleb. "I suppose she told you, just like Mallory the bastard Bledsoe told Pete about his pregnant wife. I bet they're common law, hell. I bet those two sainted folks never stood afore no altar."

"Leave it, Caleb," I say, kind of tired-like.

He laughs. Sounds like black tar ought to come out of his mouth with that laugh.

"Don't y'all remember that priest?" says Tom. "Think how he looked and how that girl looked. Now didn't they look just alike?"

"Yeah," says Caleb, laughing and drinking, "she had the biggest tits north of Monterrey. Seen 'em myself. Only I paid. Damn, Tom, whyn't she make you pay? Oughtta charged you extra for lessons too. Fourteen, hell. What could you do at fourteen?"

Tom ain't mad at all. Nothing makes Tom mad. Me, I'd of shot Caleb long since, but looking from the outside you can see Tom wins hands down every time.

"That girl were right pretty," says Tom. "Don't you recollect her, Pa? Right pretty. Lemme have another pull at that bottle, what do you say?"

Pinto hands him the bottle. He tilts his head way back and the amber stuff sloshes against the glass. Tom coughs, damn near swallows the bottle, coughs until his face goes red and his eyes run.

"Easy, boy," says Pinto.

"Easy, hell," says Tom, his throat tight from coughing, and choking on the words. "That girl stood it easy, that's what. That girl was my first, that's what."

Caleb looks down with his eyes half-closed, like his feet suddenly got real interesting. I can hear him say she's your last too, but his lips stay still, molded into that sneer, and he says it silent. Pinto hears too and looks hard at him.

"I ain't said nothing," says Caleb.

"No," Tom says gently, "you ain't."

"How's that roast cooking?" asks Pinto, and checks it himself. "We're turning into regular housemaids."

"You figure it's Christmas yet?" I ask.

"Naw," says Tom.

"What if it was?" says Caleb.

I shrug. "Seems like a break, I guess. You know, last year into next year. Seems to mark the end of something, or maybe the start."

"You're getting mighty thoughtful," says Tom.

I laugh. "Righto."

"I think you're right about the priest," says Caleb, stretching his legs. "That girl did look like him, along with half the kids in the parish. Yeah, that priest had hisself some fine times."

"Probably some fine ailments too," Pinto mutters.

The boys chuckle, then Caleb says, "How about your father, Pete? Think your pappy might've been a priest? Maybe a preacher, circuit rider? No, I heard them boys is too sainted to mess with the local women. But a priest, heh? How about that?"

"My father was a rancher."

"That so?"

"That's so."

"Y'all ever see him nowadays? Ever get home for a visit? Where's home anyway? Texas, but where?"

I think, Fuck you, Caleb. "He's been dead fourteen years, and home is wherever I make down my bed, like most folks. Now you through asking questions or do you want me to tell it all?"

Caleb looks hard at me with the skin stretched tight over his broad flat nose and the bristles of his beard poking through on his dark cheeks and chin. I feel Pinto look from one to the other of us but he keeps silent though you know he knows something's up and if Caleb were anyone else he'd ask just what. But he don't, he never will, he lets Caleb go his own way and if you search deep enough you see it makes him right sad, he's a sad old man with his best son dying and his other one on the road to a gutful of lead and no help for it, he's a sad, sad old man.

"After we eat that roast," I say, "I'm going to Bledsoes'. Y'all can stay here and if you do I'll make sure you get paid one way or the other."

So we eat the roast and onions and potatoes, and then I take a bottle of whiskey and set off in the dark on Red. Mallory Bledsoe may think whiskey turns a man bad, but this is for Sarah and if he don't like it he can go fuck himself. He can anyway.

TWENTY-THREE

This night is about as dark as the inside of a cow. You can feel the critters nearby as you ride but only your ears tuned to the low roll of the North Fork and your horse's night sense get you where you want to go. On the north bank I turn Red east and downstream a ways we bear northeast, until small squares of yellow poke through the trees: the cabin's windows. We angle toward the light, moving slow.

Still a hundred yards off I hear a scream. I haul on the reins so hard that Red rears, kicks his hooves out front, neighs.

The scream streaks through the black night, shrill as pain itself. I spin Red around, point him toward that cabin, and lay spurs to his sides.

The scream rises above the hoofbeats, thundering hoofbeats, but they can't hide it. The yellow squares seem to shrink and dim, sometimes I think the light has died but a stand of trees blackened it, a stand black as all of this night is black. I lean forward on Red, low over his neck, grip tight with my knees, force the leather saddle to suck me onto it.

Branches whip my face, my arms, my legs, bruising, and then the dark becomes the South Texas Brasada, and we streak through the brush toward the Rio Grande. Joshua rides ahead, farther ahead, I can't catch him, he moves too fast, I can't move hardly at all, ropes pull me, ropes snap tight around my arm. Snakes, not ropes. Fangs sink deep, ropelike bodies anchored eastward snap taut, yank me back, rip the flesh from my arm, rip the muscle, rip to the bone, and poison courses toward my heart, tightens my chest, yanks me eastward, always eastward.

Refugio, they named you wrong. Refugio, you mother-fucking son of a Godforsaken scrap of land, your slime so thick it bogs man and beast, your snakes so thick they coil in every corner, behind every barn, under every shrub. I hate you, Refugio. I hate your name and your men, but mostly your women, them and your snakes. I hear that rattle still, a snake's tail, clutched in a baby's hand. I hear it, I will always hear it.

Make thunder, Red, but you can't cover it, make speed and the ropes yank you back. I pull you in and those yellow squares are as small as ever, opaque yellow in an opaque night, give no light, flat, tepid, opaque; closed.

I raise my forearm to block the light. I close my eyes and listen to Red blow, listen to myself breathe. My heart thumps in my chest, I hear it push blood against my hearing, I heard it beat this way when I turned my back on Sheila McCrory as she died, turned to see Ryan Buckley dead, and in front of him Kim, alive. And between them Joshua, and the entrances to those blackrock cave eyes shut forever, and peace on his face, peace sealed those caves, peace while my heart banged in my chest, peace I saw but could not share. He took it with him like they all do, in the end, leaving none for us, spiriting their secrets beyond this world.

I lower my arm and the yellow squares are in front of me, I am there. I get off Red and the saddle leather makes its gentle creaking sound. I drop one rein to the ground and the door to the cabin opens and Mallory Bledsoe stands black against the yellow, black except where the hairless top of his head shines a little, which looks comical next to all that surrounds us and all that has gone before and goes on now. Comical, but I don't let on to laugh.

"Is that you, Jackson?"

I walk to where he can see me better. There's a noise from inside, a low moan. Mallory Bledsoe don't even look around, the bastard.

"It's near Christmas," I say. "I figured y'all might need some help."

Another low moan, then a desperate whisper: "Mallory." And still he don't turn.

I step forward. "Is she all right?"

"We don't need your help."

"I could ride for a doctor."

He stands silent, a wall of black against a wall of yellow, but there's that tiny glint off the top of his head.

"Go away," he says. "Get out and leave us be. You're a serpent in our garden. Go back to your kind."

Sarah shrieks.

I push into Mallory Bledsoe but he tries to block the way.

"Get out!" he cries. "Serpent, get out!"

He's loco for sure, loco and ought to die, but that Colt hangs straight at my hip while I lower my shoulder and slam into below his ribs, lift him clear off the floor. He crashes backward over chairs, table, lands in a heap of arms and legs, and as I run past, calls behind me, "You viper! Go back to your brood!"

I stop in the doorway to the bedroom. I can hear Bledsoe get up. I don't care. Flame sputters atop a candle on a table by the bed: the room is dim, tarnished like old brass.

Sarah lies in the middle of the bed in the middle of the room, in the candle's sputtering light, and the light turns the browned skin of her face sallow and the sheen on her skin reflects the light. Her gray eyes watch me, opaque as the yellow squares that brought me here and near drove me away, opaque as the night and the body and soul of her husband standing with his back to the light, trying to turn me away when the light failed, standing behind me now, a presence breathing over my shoulder but as dead and stiff with cold as his damn whiteface cattle will be come spring. If spring ever comes.

A tattered colorless quilt covers Sarah's belly and legs, and a thin white gown stretches across her breasts where the quilt leaves off. Her arms lie along her sides and the sinews stand out and as I look at her arm I see her fist on the near side clenched, white-knuckled.

She changes gradually, you miss it at first and then you realize the sinewy tightness spreads across her chest, up her neck. The cords of muscle stand out on her neck, the place under her sharp chin hollows, the skin stretches so tight over her chin and along her jaw you think the bones will cut through. Her cheeks hollow and grow longer and you realize she has opened her mouth. Her lips draw back and you hear her breath come in a gasp and then fast. Her eyes close, open wide, close tight and stay closed, lines at the corners, lines in her forehead.

She turns her head away, then toward you, then away and back again, presses it into the pillow, arches her neck so you think it will snap. She draws her legs up, parts her knees. The tattered, colorless quilt rises, her knees stand out sharply, small mountains. Her ballooning belly contracts, tries to squeeze the swelling loose like you'd squeeze an infected cut.

Sweat trickles down the sides of her face and neck. She moans and I go to her though what the hell I am supposed to do I do not know.

"What do I do?"

Sarah gasps, then pants. Then she screams and I want more than life itself to jump back.

"What do I do?"

Sarah's head comes off the pillow, she damn near sits up, her back round, her head near on her chest. She pushes. I lift the quilt off her legs and look and her whole self is there pushing.

A red dome stretches the parting skin, slithers out, a red-streaked face, a coin-sized hand, a tiny narrow chest. I don't know what the hell to do so I catch it and then it's in my hands and squirming, and the hole in the middle of its red-streaked face opens and out comes the most Godawful bellering I ever heard in my whole damn life.

Sarah lies back breathing hard. The kid screams in my arms and I see it's a girl. I hold my knife over the candle and cut the cord.

"What do I do with her?" I ask, kind of weakly, but when I look around at Mallory Bledsoe he turns from the doorway and disappears.

"Sarah," I say, "what the hell do I do?"

But Sarah has her eyes closed and her breathing back to normal and you'd think she fell asleep except you see the water on her face and know it ain't sweat.

I have no idea what to do and the baby screams. I find a towel and some water in the main room and clean her, then take her back to the bedroom. Sarah still has water streaming along her face, though her body don't shake and she breathes regular. I lay the baby next to her, in the crook of her arm, with its head on her shoulder. Sarah has give out a mess of blood, so I clean it up and put a dry towel under her.

I have a little trouble with all this, I think maybe I should've stayed in the dugout, or at Juniper, or Renova. Hell, I should've stayed up north four years ago when I had the chance. I got no love for Texas and why I came back I'll never know.

The baby has quieted. Sarah has never opened her eyes nor said a word, though I think she's stopped crying. Hard to tell, and I ain't wiped her face.

I go to the main room and on outside: no sign of Mallory Bledsoe.

"Bledsoe! Bledsoe, you have a girl in here!"

No answer.

I walk toward the barn, or where I recollect it to be since I can't see nothing. I near run into it, light a match, slide the door aside. Mallory Bledsoe sits on the first bench of two rows of benches with an aisle down the middle and an altar up front. There's a candle lit on the altar so the light glints off Bledsoe's head the way it done before. He has his back to me and don't turn around, and that copper-color hair hangs in wisps over his neck and between his shoulders, which shake a little, or it could be the movement of the flames from my match and his candle.

"This was to be my church," he says.

"You have a girl. You should go inside and see her."

I see his thin-haired head nod, or maybe it bows.

"My church," he whispers.

TWENTY-FOUR

Guess I better hang around. Mallory Bledsoe sits on that bench all night, all the next day and next night, and sits there now, two days after the birth. I give up trying to make him come see his baby, though it might snap him out of this spell and God knows Sarah will need someone around, even a poor locoed bastard like Mallory Bledsoe.

I range a short way from the cabin and beef a drifted heifer, cook some and carry a plate to Sarah. She lies flat with that baby girl in the crook of her arm. I fixed a cloth around the baby but Sarah don't seem to mind what mess she or the baby makes in the bed. When I take the plateful to her she acts like I ain't there.

"Look," I say, "you got this room foul and a baby to take care of. I ain't staying forever and that son of a bitch husband of yours won't leave his God damned church."

The baby stirs and her face begins to flush. I am afraid she'll let loose but she don't.

"His God damned church," Sarah murmurs. "That's very funny."

Then she opens her eyes and looks at me a few seconds before letting them fall shut again.

"You've got to get out of bed," I say. "It stinks to high heaven in here."

"Yes." Her eyes slide open again. She looks and talks real weak, like her insides have turned to old gray air.

"I ain't sure how it ought to be after a baby," I say. "You think you're all right?"

She sort of laughs, or starts to. "Yes. Take her and I'll sit in the chair. Linens are in the trunk."

She moves the baby toward me. I hold it and it squirms and waves bare puffy arms, moves its mouth as if to suck but don't cry. Wisps of red hair show on its blotchy head. I hold it in one arm and help Sarah to the bedside chair with the other. Sarah moves real stiff but don't let on to wince. Her face goes white under the sunbrowned skin as she leans back in the chair. I hand her the baby.

"She got a name?"

"No."

I set about changing the bed and feel mighty strange doing it. I can't recollect ever changing a bed before. Truth is I feel some pissed over the whole deal and expect I better get along right soon, if only Mallory Bledsoe would come in from his damn barn. Guess I'm changing the bed with kind of a vengeance because after a minute I notice Sarah watches me with a smile tugging at her lips.

"What's so funny?" I say. "Maybe you ought to do this yourself, huh? Maybe you ought to had that baby all by yourself, no one but that locoed bastard of a husband to sit in his church while you had that baby."

Now she smiles for real, first time I seen it, and I try hard to stay pissed but truth is that smile takes years off her face, and now I know why a man might incline toward looking at her twice. I seen it underneath before but now she lets it out and I have to smile myself.

"I never changed a bed before."

"It shows."

"Never delivered a baby, neither."

"I know."

I let the clean linens fall in a heap and sit on top of them on the bed, my knees near touching Sarah's.

"I think you've done a fine job," she says, "and if you want to go back to the Circle S I'm sure I can manage."

"Guess it's high time. God knows them rustlers could've run off with all the stock by now."

"Do you think they would?"

"No. Not Circle S, anyway."

"Are they very bad?"

"Only the one. Well, maybe he ain't so bad. I think he is, though."

"Do you think Mallory is very bad?"

I stand and get about finishing the bed. Ain't so hard if you work at it.

"Do you?" says Sarah.

"Here. I'm all through." I start to take her arm, to help her back to bed.

"I would like a clean nightgown."

So I dig one out of the trunk. Sarah hands me the baby again and I hand her the nightgown.

"I'll go in the other room," I say. She laughs. "Hell with it," I say, and she changes. Her belly is slack but the rest of her is firm, almost stringy, tough but supple, like a good rawhide rope. Maybe it ain't right to compare a woman's body that way, but on her it fits.

After she changes I help her to bed, her and the baby. She sets against the pillows with her hair falling tangled around her face and looks pretty worn out, but better than before; truth is, better than I seen her since we met.

"I would love a bath," she says, "just a sponge bath, but I won't ask you to do that."

"Good. I ain't no nurse."

"You've done fine."

"Righto."

"Pete?"

"Yeah?"

"When will you go back?"

I shrug. "Soon as I can get Mallory in from that barn."

"That may be never."

"Not if I drag him."

"Do you think he's very bad?"

"No."

"You are lying." She says it gently, or at least gently for her.

I shrug. "What if I am? I could think he's the worst man ever crossed the plains and it wouldn't make no nevermind. Ain't my place to say. Ain't yours to ask."

"I suppose not."

I start for the door, I figure to drag Mallory Bledsoe in here. But then I stop and turn and Sarah holds that baby girl I brung onto this Godforsaken prairie, and Sarah lets no one behind her the way her cabin's yellow windows let out no warmth nor invite no one in at night, but still I go behind all that with her, I'm back there with her, like we're two kids crouched behind a wall.

"If you want," I tell her, "I'll help you with that bath."

I leave Mallory Bledsoe to his church the rest of that day and the night that follows. Next morning Sarah eats some breakfast and even walks around a little. I have no idea how long a woman ought to stay in bed, but seems to me the best way to get well is to pretend you already are. Then Sarah tells me most women stay in bed a long time.

"All right," I say, with her leaning on my arm and the baby wriggling in the middle of the bed, "maybe you ought to lie down."

But she keeps walking.

"What're you going to name that girl?"

"I don't know yet. In a way I don't believe she's mine."

I keep silent.

We take a few more steps and Sarah says, "She looks so much like Mallory."

"Looks more like a wrinkled red plum to me."

"You don't think babies are pretty?"

"Well."

"Neither do I. But she is sweet. She hardly cries."

"I reckon."

"Men don't like babies much, do they?"

"Well, they make a lot of noise."

"This is a quiet baby, though."

"I reckon."

"Here, let me sit. What do you think I should call her?"

"Hell, I don't know."

"She'll end up with Red. I know it."

"That's my horse's name: Red."

Sarah smiles. I sit next to her on the edge of the bed. She rests her hand on my knee. Behind us the baby makes a sucking sound. I put my hand over Sarah's.

"It's time I got back."

"I know."

But I sit still.

"You'd make a wonderful nurse."

"Righto. Trail boss and nurse. Ha."

"And what else?"

"What else?"

"Yes: what else are you? I think there is more."

"Everyone has more. But not everyone needs to know about it."

"I'm not everyone."

"No, you're not."

"Well?"

"Well, I better see about your husband, that's what."

She takes away her hand, folds it in her lap with her other one. "Leave him there. I can manage alone. I'd rather manage alone."

"Then why did you marry him?"

She looks at me sharply, and now she's behind the wall and I'm outside.

"All right," I say, "I'm going to the barn."

I walk outside and the north wind slices through my shirt, stiffens my fingers. The sun shines in its weak, wintry way, like through water, and you can see a line of snow clouds on the horizon. The barn rises in front of me, the wood as bare and frigid as the pinched skin on a frostbit cheek.

I grasp the handle on the big door and slide it open, and when I close it behind me the air inside feels even colder, but still, like in a sealed cave. The lone candle on the altar has long since burned out, leaving a lumpy coat of white wax on the candle holder. Sunlight barely makes it through the cracks between the wood planks and the whole place is gray and still, with no smell of hay or beast to tell you you're anywhere but a cave or a tomb.

I walk slowly down the center aisle and the wind hisses through the cracks.

TWENTY-FIVE

I dig a cigarro from my saddlebags, and a match, stick the cigarro between my teeth, strike the match on the table. Smoke gathers nice in me, first cigarro in ages, seems like. I wave out the match. Then I dig for the bottle of old man Garth's whiskey, uncork it, set two cups on the table, pour it out.

Sarah sits in the chair by the hearth near the table, nursing the baby. She watches me pour the whiskey, watches my dirt-stained hand hold the neck of the bottle and set the cup on the edge of the table so she can reach it. She watches my hand and then she looks at the front of my shirt, but I don't plan on changing it, dirt or no dirt; it's only soil and Texas soil at that; it will only get dirty again.

I stand with the table and the nursing baby between Sarah and me. I lift my cup, drain it, let out a good deep breath.

"Long time," I say.

She nods, uncovers the other breast and covers the first one, shifts the baby. She never seems to mind my seeing.

"Don't it get sore, her sucking all the time?"

"Sometimes."

I nod, pour another whiskey. "Drink up, Sarah Bledsoe."

"I will."

I walk to the window but it's newly dark and I only see myself: scruffy, tangled, streaked with Texas soil.

"I'm wearing Texas. Damn."

She don't reply. The baby makes sucking sounds, then that stops and I hear Sarah pat her and she makes a tiny burp. I hear the fire pop and Sarah swallow and set the cup back on the table.

"More?" I ask.

"Please."

So I pour more and she drinks it. You'd think she stands it too easy, nary a sign, but then you realize the surface of her has thinned, the inside has swelled and heated and softened. You still can't see past the outside, but it's thinner than before.

"I've decided what to call the baby."

"Yeah?"

"Mallory."

I look around at her.

"It means luckless. Did you know that?"

"Mallory is a man's name."

She laughs harshly.

I walk away from the window, cork the bottle and set it on a shelf.

"You can take it with you," says Sarah.

"I cleared out the benches and the rest. The horses and two milk cows are in the barn now. I butchered you another heifer. There's enough cornmeal and such to get you through, and Mobeetie ain't far."

"I'll be all right."

I draw on the cigarro. "You know, a lot of them whitefaces won't make it to spring. It's a rough winter and you best get out now.

Maybe old man Garth has some work, maybe Rafaela needs some help running the place. Hell, old man Garth don't run that spread."

"We'll be fine," she says, but she ain't letting me behind that wall, or maybe she is and I can't go there. Hell with it. Hell with Mallory Bledsoe, the man, I mean.

"Sure you will," I say.

"Will you stop back? Now and then?"

"Sure. *Seguro.*"

She sort of smiles. "I shouldn't have asked. I'm sorry."

"I'll stop back."

"No, don't. I wish you wouldn't."

I shrug. Whatever. What the hell. Truth is I guess I better not. I take a chance and look behind her thin outside and she opens to let me in.

"Sarah—"

But the truth is there's no help for it and she can see that, but she don't push. She is a good woman for not pushing, the best woman I have known.

"How did he do it?" she asks, quiet, gentle, but not sad, or not too much.

I put on my coat and hang my saddlebags over my shoulder and heft my saddle. The saddle creaks and the creak sounds familiar but distant, like I ain't heard it in a long time. Which I ain't.

"He slit his wrists." I open the door and the cold rolls in.

TWENTY-SIX

The snow starts after Red and I cross the North Fork. It falls straight from clouds to snow-covered prairie, and you wonder what's missing. You feel it on your face, tiny pellets; you pause to listen and hear millions of pellets strike the crust, a fine sound, a sound you've never heard before but now you do. You puzzle on it, ride on, maybe pause again. You know what it is, you know something's missing. You can't figure what.

Red walks like he ain't eaten in weeks, like he's half dead. And I feel weary, like there's no breath left in me. Red goes on at the same dead pace clear to the dugout, where smoke coils from the tin-can chimney to spread and fade in the snow. No noise leaks out, and I must admit I ain't so thrilled to see that smoke. Truth is I kind of want to be on my own.

But I climb down and there they are: Pinto, Tom, Caleb. It's near midnight, I reckon, so they're strewn round the hearth half-asleep, along with a few bottles. They've pretty well shot the liquor supply, but I guess I helped.

"I done forgot how bad it smells in here," I say.

Pinto groans his way to sitting. Tom coughs and props himself on one elbow. Caleb raises his bristly chin off his chest and sneers.

"Well, well," says Caleb. "We was kind of hoping Mallory Bledsoe might've shot you."

"Mallory Bledsoe's dead."

Pinto's eyes narrow.

"I God," says Tom. "Did you kill him?"

I drop my gear and haul off my boots. "No."

"Like hell," says Caleb.

I drag him to his feet by the shirt and belt him in the jaw. I hear his jaw crack and Pinto and Tom grab me by the arms and Caleb smashes his fist into my gut.

"Caleb!" hollers Pinto. He lets me go, pushes Caleb away before he or I can swing again. I ain't for it anyway. Tom still has my arm. I shake him loose. Caleb packs an iron punch but that jaw is broke.

"Sorry, Pete," says Pinto, but not for Caleb: for holding me.

I nod. Caleb tries to work his jaw and his eyes tear some but the hate burns off the water. Tom climbs to the door, returns with an ice ball wrapped in his bandana. Caleb refuses it, never stops glaring at me. I got my wind back now but don't say nothing.

"Ain't no wind outside," says Tom, to break it. "Nary a breeze."

"I knew something was missing," I say.

"It'll pick up," says Pinto.

But it don't. Snow falls straight all night and into the next morning, when I ride the gray gelding west to check the drift. I leave before the rustlers even stir, though Pinto likely sees.

On the plains the cattle stand still: no wind to tell them where to go. They stand still and silent, statues in pale colors with white backs and white fringing the tops of their horns, and mixed among them a few brick red coats, dying already, dying because they stand still, hooves on one crust of snow, new snow halfway up their legs. I sit the gray, warm inside my buffalo robe, and watch the cattle die.

"Drift, you beasts," I tell them. "You stupid fucking beasts."

But they stand still and the snow falls straight and gentle now, like lace, and I sit and watch until out of the lace comes the high tin tinkle of a bell and then a team of black horses and a sleigh behind, making for all the world like they come right through a lace curtain, and a bundled figure on the sleigh, whip held high.

I ride toward the sleigh and under the bundle I see Rafaela. She reins in her team and I rein in the gray.

"Howdy," I say. "How come you're out here?"

She looks at me through those pine-color eyes, coolly. "It's Christmas, or it was yesterday. I brought you supplies and a feast."

"You drive all night? What about old man Garth?"

"He's been ill for some months now. Ever since you left." She scans the range.

"Circle S stock are south," I say. "Long since."

"Yes. Are those the squatter's Herefords?"

"Yup."

She nods slowly. "I suppose there's little point in you staying out here. You ought to finish the winter at headquarters. I'll still pay you, of course."

I chuckle.

"You may stay in the main house."

"Andy never knew you at all, did he?"

"No. But we had fun, a long time ago."

We start for the dugout, but I have to know something. I think, should I ask or not, but I have to know. So I pull up and she does too.

"Can you tell me something?" I ask her.

Her lips curl up a little. She has full lips and white teeth and her lips are painted red. She has high cheekbones that slant her eyes and she looks at me through the pine green of her eyes, out from under those half-closed lids and black lashes. She stops that sleigh in the middle of a part of the prairie with acres of nothing but snow all around, not even a beast except on the west horizon and only the trees, a line of gray, faint in the north. She is bundled in layers of fur but you know she'd smolder stark naked in a blizzard.

"You are Garth's woman, right?"

"I have been, yes."

I look off west for a minute. "Okay, then. Are you his daughter, too?"

"I have never known, but I think not. But if you insist on virtue, let me ask: did you really kill your father?"

"I did. When I was thirteen."

"And you offer no reason?"

"You want a reason?"

"Yes."

"He beat my brother to death."

"And your mother, what did she do?"

"She shot me. And then she put out a reward."

She nods. "That's what I thought. Will you ever go back?"

"Back? What for?"

"To clear your name. You can't hide any longer, you know. As a trail boss you are too well known. People have started to add up the stories. Henry Clayton came to the ranch, he trailed you there and I sent him away. Did you know he was trailing you? Did you know he was a Ranger?"

"Sure," I say. "Of course."

We have pretty much of nothing more to say, so we travel east with a blanket of white on our furs and the snow still falling straight but thinner. I wish to hell the wind would start: no new air to breathe and I feel smothered. After awhile the dugout comes into view but no smoke this time, that chimney looks like an old empty tin can some lone traveler left behind, like it looked the day I arrived.

I climb down into the dank room while Rafaela waits under her furs in the sleigh, and damn if there ain't a sign of them three rustlers, nary a sign. Except maybe a scent lingers, though it could be in my mind, and the liquor's down to nothing, so I guess they took the last three bottles.

"Damn," I say, kind of surprised.

I sit cross-legged in front of the cold hearth, poke the ashes with a stick. Charred lumps sit on top of the ashes, chip apart when I jab them.

"Damn," I say again, and the cold air and flurries of snow tumble through the open trapdoor and onto my back, and I can even feel it through that buffalo robe, or I think I can.

After awhile I hear Rafaela on the ladder but I keep facing the cold dead hearth.

She asks what I am doing and I shrug, I make no reply, and inside I wonder if maybe I'm going a little loco.

"Why are you sitting there?" says Rafaela right behind me. "Aren't you going to help unload the sleigh?" She pauses. "Did you drink all that whiskey?"

"No. I had help. And no need to unload."

"Then you'll come back to the main house."

I shake my head. "Naw, I figure I'll head out."

"Out?"

"Yeah, south. Guess I'll head south."

She's quiet for a spell. I get to my feet and my joints creak. Maybe I'm getting old again but I only feel dead, like that hearth or the windless prairie. The whole world outside has lost its breath and its color, gone to white and black but mostly gray.

"I think I'll head south," I say again.

She watches me like I just beat her at something, but damn if I know what. She looks some pissed but don't let on much, as is her way.

"The money is at the house," she says.

"Money?"

"To pay you. For the last four months' work."

"Oh."

"You do want to be paid."

"Sure, why not." I think about Pinto and the boys and whether they might come back to the dugout for wages. Well, they can always have their pick of cattle, especially since there's no Circle S stock up here anymore.

"I'd rather rest before starting back," says Rafaela, but she looks around the dugout like she'd rather rest somewhere else. I guess it could stand a good airing.

"There's a cabin across the river. River's froze hard enough in places to hold the sleigh. Widow name of Sarah Bledsoe lives in the cabin."

"Will you come over?"

"I'll show you the best place to cross."

"And the money?"

I shrug. "Think I'll just head south. Hold it for me, okay?"

She gives me something like twelve dollars from her purse and we go back outside. I close off the mangy dugout for the last time and think I best fill it in. But hell, leave it. I switch my saddle to Red, pack a few provisions. Rafaela says she'll lead the other two horses to pasture nearer the main house. I climb on Red.

We head through the straight-falling snow into the trees, toward the part of the North Fork with the thickest ice. At the river you can see across to Sarah's land but not to the cabin, not even with the trees bare. I reckon that's just as well. In my mind, though, I'd swear I can hear that little baby girl with the wispy red hair cry. Then I realize the wind has started, finally.

Rafaela slips graceful fingers from a leather glove and we shake hands.

"I had hoped you would take a herd north this spring," she says. "I still do."

I smile, let go of her hand. She flicks the whip and the black team paces off, hooves clicking on the ice, bells tinkling. I see her safely across, turn Red and ride out south, before the wind.

TWENTY-SEVEN

I don't know where I am riding, except south, but as the snow thins to nothing and spiky brown grass pokes through, then gives way to rock and cactus and sand, I know where I am, or should be, but not where it ends. I try to think of something else.

With the wind Red came back to life. Or life came back to Red. Without the wind the prairie grass points at the sky and the sky hates the grass, usually, bakes it, sometimes floods it, sends lightning to burn it. The grass points straight at its tormentor and dies. But when the wind starts the grass takes to waving.

I do not know where I am going. I never have. I should turn around and go to Sarah and that little baby. I helped bring that baby into the world and that was a good thing I done, but I could do no good for Sarah, not in a world full of men like Henry Clayton and boys like Caleb, not when everyone in Texas knows me before I ever climb down and introduce myself.

Howdy, I'm Pete Jackson.

Yeah, I know.

Everybody knows. Except it's Peter Jack Costello, or no one would turn his head.

You know, I wanted to work cattle since I could see over the sides of the cradle, and I wanted to trail them north since the outlets opened. I never asked nothing else and I got my wish. Maybe I should've asked for more. Now I have a bad feeling about driving north: you can sense the end of it, sniff it on the breeze, you could smell it this fall with the first of the drift, or before, when the horses' coats thickened early and the grass stood froze against the wind, waiting.

What do I have when it ends?

Well, I could hole up at Renova, work the horses, the black bulls, the ladinos in the brush. I could hammer out small-time deals with small-time operators on the Texas side. Hell, I could catch a rustler or two, maybe bust some bigger rings, impress the Rangers.

Hell with that.

But I could work on Renova. If I want to. Truth is I'd rather think of anything but retracing my steps, God knows life's enough trouble once around without redoing what you've got out of the way. God knows. Funny, but my mother used to say that. I mean about going around twice. My mother had it twice as hard as any woman, with my father's hand always at her face. Strikes me as amazing she had any face left.

Red lopes under me, south, south, and I still don't know why that woman leveled that gun at me and pulled that trigger, after all the times his hand bruised her cheek. I don't know why she offered the reward. I don't know how she could have missed him enough to do it; I have never missed him at all, only my brother Mick; I have spent years missing Mick, or trying not to think about missing Mick.

Seems to me that nothing lasts, that even the parts of your life that beat strongest and closest to what you are, to your deepmost self, that even those parts you better be ready to let go, because nothing lasts. Seems so, anyhow.

So if I don't know where I'm going at least Red remembers the way. We retrace our steps, and though I've held every grain of Texas soil close at some point I think now how it all looks so foreign: I came back to Texas four years ago and I'll never know why, because I got no love for it any more than any place else, and if I had half a brain I'd light out for north, Alberta maybe, what the hell.

But I ride south. And when I did ride north I stopped short of the border. Ha, I had that dugout smack on the east border and that endless fence kept me inside. Two strands of bobwire I could step between so neatly, but I only went over if I had to, on business so to speak.

When the cattle stop trailing and the whitefaces crowd out the rangy, ornery, wild beasts we call longhorns, Texas will have changed but she will still be Texas. And if I rot in jail for what I done my feet will still rest on Texas. I have never loved any piece of ground but I cannot leave here and know I will never come back, unless I have found something else, something better.

"Hey, Red," I say, and pull up short, and from where we stand on the South Rim of the Chisos you can see way down into Juniper Canyon and across the Rio, into the mountains on the Mexican side. Juniper and sage roll over rock pounded to sand, roll in waves of green, from pine-color to prairie green to the gray of Sarah Bledsoe's eyes; you could never see into Sarah, though I could get behind the gray with her, she let me do that, and I swear I can see into her right now, here at the head of Juniper Canyon.

And into myself too, though maybe a man were meant to know only the outside of himself and make up the inside, and know only the outside of folks, and so he's free, and so he's alone. But then you have places like Juniper and women like Sarah.

"Maybe we come too far south," I say to Red, who tosses his long black mane.

But we keep going, we ride over the Sierras to San Fernando, and of course San Fernando ain't changed: women wrapped in rebozos sit out front of low jacales on the one dusty street, old or looking old; chickens squawk and scatter, a passel of dogs forms from the dust to yap and take the horse's tail in the face, leap and nip if they find the energy, lose interest, crawl back to sun on the street. Kids peer around corners, call in Spanish, maybe a couple step forward to stare from big dark eyes, the whites like snow in brown faces, or narrowed if they're a little older, a little more savvy.

San Fernando will never change, in all of history: the monastery on the hill will watch forever and there will always be a priest and a whore and a ranchero.

Mercedes waits for me outside her cantina, watches me ride on my blazing red chestnut stallion down the street, through the chickens and dogs and children. Mercedes folds her arms under her big melon-round breasts that swell her woollen dress, and she juts one hip and cocks her head to the side while her long black hair catches the sun, glows redly under the black, spreads in curls over her shoulders.

"Well, Costello," she says when I stop Red in front of her, "where have you been?"

"The Chisos. Juniper."

"All of this time?"

"The beginning and the end."

"And now?"

I shrug and slide off Red but I do not embrace Mercedes and she makes no move toward me.

"Now I'm here. You got anything to drink?"

She smiles with her lips closed. "*En español,* Costello."

We go inside. She uncorks some Jack's, pours it for both of us. The cantina is swept but you can smell the night before.

"Is today Sunday?" I ask, in Spanish.

"*Sí.*"

I smile. The whiskey tastes good, feels better. I used up Rafaela's twelve dollars long since: so much for whiskey. Mercedes pours more. She has not touched me.

"What did you do in between?" she asks.

"Worked up north."

"Oh. You stayed in Texas."

"Maybe I always will."

She laughs: that single "Ha," as usual.

"You do not think so?" I say, but she don't reply. I down another whiskey and finally ask if Kim is still around.

Later, as the sun turns red and slips behind slats of purple clouds, fading, returning, fading, like peeking through a fence, I ride to Renova. I wait in the courtyard in the gathering dusk and wonder why they let me wait so long. It's okay, though: I lean on the railing and smoke a cigarro, listen to the parrots' polite Spanish and the water trickling from the Virgin's fountain.

The sky above the courtyard turns to an evening blue you can see into, that gets darker the farther in you look, and the greenery of the courtyard melts together, shadowy, so the statue shimmers white against it, the lines blur, so that if you look long enough without blinking she turns grainy. You listen to the water and the parrots until they sound as ghostlike as the Virgin looks, so you strain to hear what is real: the yip of a coyote, the distant bellow of a black Spanish bull, the rustle under the plants that could be a desert rat or a snake.

There's a small booted step on the wood floor behind me and when I turn the whitish bundle in this small woman's arms glows as ghostlike as that statue.

"Don Vicente thought I should see you first," says Kim.

I let my cigarro fall and it makes a gentle sound hitting the wood. I crush it out, but gently. I nod in what is now the dark.

"Will you light the lantern?" she asks in her same husky boyish voice.

So I light one of the lanterns on the wall. I cannot see the baby because of its wrappings. I have no idea what to say, at first. Then I do.

"Joshua knew?"

She nods. I look into her and wonder that she don't seem to hate me. I want to ask why she didn't tell me before I left, but asking that would be wrong and I know why anyhow.

"His name is Joshua." She holds him toward me. I take him and he squirms in my arms but goes on sleeping. In the faint gold light of the lantern he looks as dark as Joshua but he is my son: I can feel it.

"I don't want you to stay," says Kim. "You know that. I work for Don Vicente; he treats the boy like his own. You know you can't stay."

For a minute I turn from her and bow my head low over this little boy, who sleeps, who may never know his father.

"I never come here to stay." I hand the baby back to Kim.

"Where to now?" she asks.

"Maybe Alberta," I say, but I am thinking of those whitefaces in the Red River breaks.